The Search for the Tinker Chief

THE SEARCH FOR THE TINKER CHIEF

by

BRÍD MAHON

With illustrations by
William Bolger

ALLEN FIGGIS : DUBLIN, 1968

MADE AND PRINTED IN THE REPUBLIC
OF IRELAND BY CAHILL & CO. DUBLIN

CONTENTS

For my nephews Stephen and Conor and all the boys and girls who like a bit of magic

THE SEARCH FOR THE TINKER CHIEF

By *Bríd Mahon*

And the Queen, jealous of the beauty of Princess Fionnula, took her four step-children—three boys and the girl—down to the waters of the lake and bade them bathe in the water. And there she turned them into swans. By the bonds of their enchantment they were compelled to spend three hundred years on Lake Darvrach, three hundred years on the Sea of Moyle in the far north, and three hundred years on the waters of Erris on the Western seaboard. This is one of the three sorrows of Irish storytelling.

CHAPTER ONE

NOVEMBER EVE

When Conor woke up on November Eve, he knew at once that it was one of those strange days when almost anything could happen.

His toes stuck out from under the bedclothes, and for a moment he thought they had turned to gold. But it was only the sun streaming through the window, throwing a golden bar of light across the bed.

All night long he had been dreaming of the bonfire on the mountains. A wild tinker man with long black hair and a gold bracelet on his arm, kept dancing in and out of his dreams. Only now it was all mixed up in his mind, and he couldn't rightly remember what it was all about.

Conor was small and brown-haired. He had lots of freckles and he could wriggle one ear. He could also play the harmonica. The night before in bed, he had practised all the tunes he could remember for bonfire night.

The bonfire was always held on the flat-topped mountains on November Eve. From his bed Conor could see that they were covered with mist. Sometimes the mist came down for days, and then the mountains were dangerous.

"If it doesn't lift, everything will be spoiled," he thought dismally. He twisted around to see better, and fell out of the wrong side of the bed. Then he put his shoes on the wrong feet, and when he went to measure himself against a mark he had on the wall, he discovered he had shrunk. Even when he stood on his toes, he couldn't quite reach up to the pencil line.

Down in the kitchen his grandmother was ladling porridge into blue delph dishes, and the hens were squawking at the door for food, the same as they did every morning. But Bran was missing from his place beside the fire. Always when Conor sat down at the table, his dog got up from the fire, and settled himself beside the chair.

"Where's Bran?" asked Conor glumly, pouring sugar over his porridge.

His grandmother took the bowl away. "Don't use it all," she said mildly. She sat down and poured herself out a cup of tea. "That dog went out last night and never came back."

Conor leaned over to take a slice of bread and upset the milk. His grandmother sighed as she wiped it up. "No doubt about it but you are a misery this morning. I thought you would be jumping out of your skin and the school closed for the turf gathering."

"What good is it if we don't have the bonfire tonight?" The cottage door was open, and Conor could see the mist was still swirling around the mountain tops.

All that morning as he helped his grandmother, and later when he went over to the bog, the feeling stayed with him that the day had turned inside out. It was nothing you could put your finger on. He lost two of his best conking chestnuts, but even that and the fact that he had grown smaller overnight, or that he had put his shoes on the wrong feet when he got up, didn't explain it. These are ordinary every-day things, and even Bran had often gone on a jaunt before. Though it must be admitted that he had never before stayed away all night.

Filling his creels with turf he tried to tell his best friend Red Rinty about his dream. "The tinker was chasing me and

he had this gold bracelet," but Red Rinty had wild red hair and he never listened to anyone.

"If I see the tinkers at the bonfire I'll scatter them," he

boasted, and Conor said disgustedly, "Maybe we won't have a bonfire at all, the way the mist is settling in. Besides, the tinkers haven't been around for ages."

As they worked on the bog, the sun came out and slowly the mist melted away. When the baskets were full, Conor swung two across the donkey's back and started for home. The donkey was stubborn and kept stopping to eat patches of nettles; Conor thought he would never get home to see if Bran had returned.

A gust of wind blew into the kitchen when he opened the door and the sparks danced. His grandmother was taking a currant cake off the fire and she looked lonely. "Bran always barks when that happens," she said. "He never came back all day."

Eating a speckled brown egg, Conor thought about his dog. "It was this time last year I found Bran at the bonfire," he said. "I think he ran away from the tinkers. I hope he hasn't gone back to them. I was dreaming about them all night, and they had a gold bracelet."

"Mind that now," said his grandmother, but no more than Red Rinty, she wasn't really listening to him. She didn't like the idea of Conor going up to the bonfire without the protection of his dog. But then everyone in the parish went, and they were all friends.

When Conor finished his tea, he took his coat and cap from a nail behind the door, and his harmonica off the kitchen dresser and went outside.

He whistled for his dog, but nothing happened. Bran was funny and no mistake. Most of the time he was as good as gold, but then for no reason at all he would become wild and unbiddable and when that happened there was no holding him.

Outside the cottage door, Conor paused to button up his coat. Away in the west the evening clouds were gathering, and the wind was whistling and rushing about. The hens were in bed in the barn, but the cock was still sitting on the wall. He was very cantankerous, and only went to bed when it suited him to do so.

Just beyond the cross-roads the boys were waiting. Red Rinty was waltzing around, waving his arms like a windmill in full sail. "Give us a bit of music," he shouted, as Conor came up. "The bonfire is lighting on the mountains. I was up there already, and the crowds were coming in from all over the place. Your old dog was there too, running around with the tinkers, like a mad thing."

"Why didn't you bring him back with you?" demanded Conor furiously, but Red Rinty only laughed. "He's old enough to know his own way, besides he was enjoying himself."

They took the lake road that led to the foot of the hills, laughing and jostling as they went along. Only Conor trailed behind kicking the white stones in the dust, his mind on his dog. "Isn't he the stupid animal getting lost," he thought.

The road turned right at the lake. Beyond that it climbed sharply between great rocky boulders. Conor paused to spin a flat stone. He could send it further than anyone else. It made four arcs before it sank in the middle of the lake. Four swans rose up and went flying over the hills.

"That's strange," said Conor, watching the flight of the swans into the sunset. The boys paid no heed to him, only moved away. Old people said that it was in this very lake that the Children of Lir had been turned into swans by their stepmother, who was a witch. Ever since birds had avoided the lake.

Conor picked up another stone and sent it skimming; then something shot between his legs and sent him sprawling. When he got to his feet, he saw his dog Bran, swimming out to the middle of the lake. Then Bran dived and came back at great speed, carrying something between his teeth.

Conor backed away from the edge, for Bran was shaking himself and the water was flying in all directions. Then he saw what his dog had laid at his feet. It was a large bracelet almost as big as a dog's collar. It was wet and slimy, but when he rubbed it in his coat, he saw it was gold, with strange markings like the heads and tails of curious animals.

"It's the bracelet I was dreaming about," he said, "only the tinker man was wearing it."

Bran wouldn't listen. He shook himself and ran away to chase a rabbit.

The mountains were turning from blue to purple, and away on the top, sparks of flame shot into the sky. Half way up Red Rinty and his companions twisted and climbed in single file, like a line of ants.

Behind a boulder something moved and Bran barked angrily. But Conor didn't notice. He danced along throwing the bracelet up in the air and catching it on his arm. Then with a wild cry a tinker boy jumped from behind the rock and went scrambling over stones and gorse up the mountains. And Conor, with his dog at his heels, followed the path Red Rinty had taken to the bonfire.

CHAPTER TWO

THE COMING OF KATHLEEN

High on the mountain-tops, Conor and Red Rinty and the boys were having the time of their lives. Bran was mad with excitement, chasing around with a pack of dogs from the far side of the bog. "I found a valuable bracelet in the lake," he boasted to a black and white mongrel. "It would be far more to the point if you found a couple of meaty bones," the dog barked back.

Boys and girls were dancing around the bonfire; an old man was sitting on a sack fiddling for all he was worth, and by the light of the flames an old tinker woman was telling fortunes to anyone who would cross her palm with silver.

"There's great adventure coming your way," she said to Conor. "Cross my hand with sixpence and I'll tell you all about it." Conor only laughed and ran by to gather potatoes to roast in the ashes.

When the dancing was finished an old man told them a story that was as old as the hills themselves. It was all about enchantment and magic and of how the King of Ireland's son had fought a giant, crossed a burning mountain on an eagle's back, rescued a Princess and lived in a glass tower.

One by one the stars had come out. Frost glittered on the grass, and the night was so cold you could see your breath. Everyone was quiet. Conor took out his harmonica and began to play a gay little tune. Then a fiddler and melodeon-player took up the music. They swung into a wild jig, and as if in answer, a band of tinkers came running across the mountains to join in the dancing.

A girl with long black hair and a red petticoat pulled Conor to his feet, and swung him around—then suddenly let go of him. A tinker man with a handsome face and hoops of gold in his ears caught Conor. A crowd of people were dancing around him and he fought to get free. The dark man with the ear-rings and yellow scarf was singing at the top of his voice:

"Oh I am the King of the Tinkers bold
And I walk with a ring of silver and gold."

And then everyone joined in:

"He travels the road with a careless swagger
Afraid of no man, king or beggar."

Then someone gave Conor a push and he staggered and tripped over Bran who had been rolling around with the tinker dogs. Together they rolled down the mountainside, and the song and the laughter of the crowd followed them.

A withered thornbush broke Conor's fall. He bumped his head and the stars danced. Then he picked himself up, slowly and gingerly. He was still clutching his harmonica, but his coat was missing. He whistled for his dog—but Bran had vanished. Tears of anger came in his eyes, but he blinked them back. "I'm fed up with this place," he shouted crossly. The words came echoing back and far away the tinkers raised a cheer.

The road home had never seemed so long or so lonely. The wind whistled past his ears, and his shirt billowed out behind him, as he raced along. He could see the light shining in the kitchen window, long before he reached the gate. The chickens and hens were all in bed, but the old cock was keeping watch on the wall. He crowed a welcome, but Conor paid no heed—and the cock went grumbling into bed, "Not a word to throw to a bird."

Conor opened the door with such force that the wind blew down the chimney and the sparks danced. His grandmother was sitting in her rocking-chair placidly knitting a sock. At her feet Bran was sleeping peacefully.

"The dog came home before you," his grandmother said smugly, "but I told him you wouldn't be long after."

Conor did a little dance with rage. "I was nearly killed. Look at the sight of me. My coat is lost and a valuable gold bracelet. Watchdog how are you."

Bran pretended to snore, and the old woman pushed her glasses down on her nose, and said shortly. "You look as if

you were in a fight right enough, but you'll live. Maybe you might close the door after you—or did you bring a visitor with you?"

Conor turned around. Standing behind him was a dark-haired girl about his own age. She hung her head shyly, and held out his coat. "I brought it back to you." Conor snatched it away and she began to cry.

The old woman got up from her seat and brought the girl to the fire. "Hush," she said, "crying won't help at all. Come over and warm yourself and tell me your name."

The little girl stopped sobbing and went over to the old woman. "My name is Kathleen. I live with the tribe, but I have no mother nor father. The tinker chief found a gold bracelet when they were all dancing, but I think it belongs to the boy." Then she held up her chin. "I'm a tinker," she said timidly.

"And what's wrong with that," said the old woman. "Aren't they decent people the same as the rest of us. Only the tinker chief is a bit wild."

From the dresser the old woman took down two blue dishes and from a pot on the hearth she ladled out helpings of porridge. "Sit up to the table now and have some supper. Tomorrow we'll see what's to be done." She turned sharply to Conor. "Wash the dirt off your hands and face and mind your manners."

Sheepishly Conor did as he was bid. He sat opposite Kathleen and they both started to giggle. Bran put his paws on Kathleen's knees and then sat down beside her chair. While they ate the old woman took out her thimble and thread and began to mend the holes in Conor's jacket.

When supper was finished Kathleen washed the dishes and swept away the crumbs. Conor settled Bran in his box for the night. Soon the old woman was yawning and slowly she wound the battered alarm clock.

"It's time for bed, children. Kathleen can sleep in your bed, Conor. You can sleep on the settle. Tomorrow we'll see what's to be done."

Kathleen's eyes were bright. You wouldn't know if it was

the firelight or something else was the cause. "You're good to me, ma'am, and I'll not forget it."

The wrinkled hand patted Kathleen's curls. "You need a home, and someone to take care of you. I'll go to my room now and say my prayers. It takes me a long time, for I've gathered a lot with the years. Good-night now and don't stay up too late."

Conor sat on a stool gazing into the flames. In the red coals he could see the Tinker Chief, head thrown back, ear-rings jingling, the gold bracelet on his brown arm. "I'll get even with him yet," he muttered half to himself. "If only I knew where they were making for?"

"I think they're going to the Fair of Belmullet."

"I'd love to follow them." In the yellow flames Conor was watching the long trek of the tinker carts and caravans over the rutted roads.

Kathleen cupped her face and her eyes too were on the fire. "Would you be game to go. I'd go with you, but your granny would never let you away."

"I'd slip off without telling her. I'd leave a note."

The tick-tock of the clock was louder. The pictures in the fire crumbled and were white ash. "Will you come tomorrow at daybreak?"

"I will. It's a bargain." And solemnly they shook hands.

Outside on the mountains the people trampled the white ash of the bonfire under foot and made for home. Red Rinty, coming down the mountains, grumbled, "That Conor . . . He let us down badly going off like that. Himself and his old harmonica. I'll give him the telling of this tomorrow when I see him."

But little did he know that many a day was to elapse and many a strange happening take place before they would all meet again.

CHAPTER THREE

THE LEPRECHAUN

It was dark, the inky darkness that comes just before dawn breaks, when Kathleen crept down the stairs and into the still-warm kitchen. Conor was sitting by the side of the settle bed with his coat on. By the light of a little red lamp he wrote a note:

Dear Gran,

Kathleen and I are going in search of the Tinker Chief. When we find the bracelet we'll both come back. Don't worry about us, we'll be all right. Take care of yourself and don't catch cold. Red Rinty will break the sticks and do the messages for you.

Love,

Conor.

Meanwhile Kathleen cut some sandwiches and wrapped them in paper. Conor put the note behind the blue china jug on the dresser, the place where his grandmother would be sure to find it. Then Kathleen and he went out into the chilly world which was now neither day nor night.

Outside the door they paused to put on their shoes, then they went softly up the garden path and out onto the road.

Bran was sitting waiting, and he wagged his tail impatiently as if to say, "Hurry up. It's about time." But he never raised his voice to bark.

"You're not coming with us, Bran," said Conor firmly. "We're going a great distance and you'd only be in the way."

Bran cocked a scornful eye at this and went galloping down the road. With a little sigh Conor followed him.

"That dog. When he makes up his mind about a thing there's no changing him."

"I wonder how he knew our plans?"

"That dog knows your thoughts before you utter them." Conor had often heard his grandmother say this.

As they turned a corner the wind caught them, whipping the ends of Kathleen's thin coat and poking icy fingers up Conor's sleeves. Kathleen pushed the hair out of her eyes and shivered.

"I wish the sun would come out. It's so cold."

Conor looked around excitedly. "I was never out so early before."

"I often was," said Kathleen, a trifle boastfully. She minced along, her steps matching her tone. "Sometimes the tinkers leave a district in the middle of the night. Wouldn't it be grand though to be riding along in a little caravan with lace curtains on the window."

"And a red hall-door, and wheels painted blue." Conor fancied these colours. "I wonder where the Tinker Chief is by now?"

"He had a good start on us." Kathleen frowned in thought. "The tinkers can travel fast when they want to. They'll probably pitch camp outside the next big town."

Somewhere there was a chattering sound as if a river had joined hands with the road. A white mist was swirling around in a fantastic dance. Kathleen clutched at Conor's hand and he whispered:

"We're beside the Yellow Bridge. We'll go down under for shelter and eat our sandwiches." Then he wondered why he was whispering, cleared his throat and said in a bossy tone, "Come along!"

Bran was running around in little circles, appearing and disappearing in the mist like a Cheshire cat. He seemed to be enjoying himself enormously. He shot down a steep path, and Conor followed, pulling Kathleen with him. Pebbles were in her shoes and the swirling mist was in her eyes. "Careful Conor, or we'll end up in the water. Take it easy."

The ground suddenly gave way and they slipped down the

incline to the water's edge. A large flat stone stopped them. They sat down on this, and Kathleen took the sandwiches out of her pocket.

Bran barked, and as if in answer, out of the mist came the sound of running footsteps, then a reedy voice commenced to whistle, *The Leprechaun.* Kathleen caught Conor's arm. "Listen to that."

"I can't see a stim," complained Conor. "It's such a queer light."

The footsteps and the whistling ceased as suddenly as they had begun. The children waited breathlessly. Then Conor had a brainwave. He pulled the harmonica out of his pocket and began to play the tune of the whistler. Softly Kathleen hummed the words, while Bran kept time by beating his tail against a stone:

"In a shady nook one moonlight night
  A leprechaun I spied
With coat of green and shoes of red,
  A cruiskeen by his side.
'Twas tick-tock-tick, his hammer went
  Upon a tiny shoe.
Oh I laughed to think of the crock of gold
  But the fairy was laughing too."

There was a peal of laughter, like a ripple of glass bells, then a reedy voice said:

"The music is grand, but it's bad to be out before your breakfast."

"Would you like a sandwich." Almost before Kathleen had finished, a little brown hand shot out of the mist and disappeared with the bread. There was silence for a while, then Kathleen called out. "It's a pity we haven't a cup of tea to give you. Bread on its own is dry, and it's cold so early in the morning."

Conor sighed so deeply that the sound seemed to come up from his boots. "I'd love a cup of tea. I'd almost go home for one."

There was a chuckle from the unseen visitor, and the little voice said, "You can have something better, so stop complaining."

"What do we . . ." began Conor, but Bran was running around kicking two tin cans.

"Dip them in the river," ordered the little voice. The mist swirled and thickened as Conor and Kathleen bent down and scooped up a drink. Whatever it was it tasted delicious. It was like tea, only sweeter. Then again it might have been soup. It was neither too hot nor too cold and it gave a grand tingling feeling inside, a feeling that made the children glow all over. Bran gave a plaintive bark, and Kathleen gave him what remained in her tin. He lapped up every drop.

"That was the nicest drink I ever had," said Conor draining his can. "I do believe the water in the river is enchanted," said Kathleen.

"Before the dawn breaks the whole world is enchanted," said the voice in the mist.

Conor moved forward in the direction of the voice, but the mist like thick fingers pushed him back. "Who are you? Are you a leprechaun?"

"Maybe I am." The voice was becoming fainter, or perhaps the mist was thicker.

"Then tell us where we'll find the Tinker Chief," pleaded Kathleen.

The mist was lifting and the tiny reedy voice seemed to lift with it, but faintly Kathleen could catch the words:

"When you come to the place where three roads meet
Ask the Stone Man to direct your feet."

Nearby a cock began to crow. The mist melted before the sunrise and the river suddenly came to life and began to run and ripple over the stones.

Kathleen sounded wistful. "The little man is gone. Now we'll never see him again."

"My grannie says they vanish at cock-crow. They go like a puff of wind just before the dawn. What were the last words the little man said, Kathleen?"

Kathleen repeated them and sighed. "Though dear knows what he meant at all."

Bran had remained very quiet, but now he jumped up and went racing along the incline and across the Yellow Bridge. Conor caught hold of Kathleen and they both followed the dog.

CHAPTER FOUR

THE ROSY WOMAN

The sun shone brightly and warmly as they walked along. A rabbit suddenly shot across their path and disappeared down a hole before Bran could reach him. A white cat washing her face on a low wall gave a friendly miaow as they passed, and then mysteriously disappeared. A spaniel sniffing along, decided to walk with them as far as the cross-roads, and then ran into a cottage with a crooked chimney and a green and yellow door.

It was a grand morning, more like June than November, and the children felt excited and happy. Bran played games like chasing spiders on the bushes and talking to cows in the fields. Sometimes he rolled on the ground with all four paws up, then again he hobbled along on two paws like an old man going the roads. When Conor put a cap on the dog, Kathleen laughed until her sides ached.

But as the day wore on, even Bran tired, and now he was trotting along as sedately as the two children. They were all glad when they heard the clip-clop of a horse, and even better pleased when a brightly-painted caravan, driven by a rosy-cheeked woman, came into view. She leaned sideways and looked down.

"You look a wee bit tired. Would you like a ride?" Her voice was kind and her blue eyes friendly.

Indeed the children were glad of the offer, though neither would pretend they were tired.

She pulled at the reins. "Hi there, Jock. Hi there, boy." She bent down a little. "Give me you hand, little girl—there you are. And now you, young fellow."

With a leap Bran was up beside Conor. The rosy woman moved sideways and tidied her grey shawl about her. "Now

we're all set and comfortable." She tugged once more at the reins. "Gee-up, Jock. Gee-up like a good horse."

The black horse flicked his well-kept mane, lifted a daintily-shod hoof and went clip-clopping down the road. Kathleen knew and loved horses, for in Ireland the tinkers spend most of their time buying and selling animals. She knew the black horse was a thoroughbred, and longed to drive the yellow caravan.

Conor said nothing for a time, then he sighed deeply. "I'm hungry. I'm simply starving."

At this Bran barked in sympathy. The rosy-cheeked woman laughed and reined the horse in beside a clearing. "I'd like a bit of dinner myself. Won't you have a bite with me."

"We'd be glad to, ma'am," said Kathleen meekly, while Conor brightened at the prospect. "We were up and out early."

"You're going a distance," the rosy woman asked as she clambered down.

"We're making for the Fair in the next big town," said Kathleen, helping her unyoke the animal.

The woman clucked in sympathy. "Musha then you have a long trek before you. But no matter, you'll be there sometime. You're both young with all the time in the world before you."

"I don't suppose you saw a sign of a tinker tribe and you on the road?" asked Conor.

"I did indeed. They passed me on the road and stopped long enough to sell me a tin basin and two tin mugs."

She released the trace and Kathleen did the same at her side. The caravan settled a little on its wheels.

The black horse wandered off in search of a patch of clover, and the children followed the woman into the caravan and helped her to lift the pots and pans out of the covered shelves. She gave Bran a mutton bone and he ran away into a corner to eat in peace.

"Did the tinkers say anything?" Kathleen was taking three cups from their hooks on the dresser.

"I had a chat with old Mary Ward," confided the rosy woman.

"And what did she say?" questioned Kathleen.

The rosy woman paused and folded her arms. "Strange talk she had of a bracelet that had come into the possession of the Tinker Chief. It was going to make all their fortunes."

"Did she say anything else, ma'am. It's very important to Conor here and myself."

The rosy woman sat down on a stool and thought hard. Conor looked out of the door at the peaceful glade, thought of his grandmother at home and wondered if all this were a dream. But the rosy woman had remembered.

"Let me see now, if I can recall her exact words. It was a kind of rhyming riddle, she spoke, something like this." The rosy woman cleared her throat and chanted:

"Where the wild ash grows
And the tawny brake
Where the mountains rise
O'er the Silver Lake

Where the tarn and stream
Run and leap and trill
Where the mountain goat
Climbs the grey-blue hill

In a sheltered spot
Which is known of old
There at last we'll find
The fairy gold."

"What in the world did she mean?" wondered Kathleen.
"And where on earth is the place?" asked Conor.

The rosy woman shook her head slowly. "I have no idea, but this much I do know. The Tinker Chief recognised the place. When old Mary Ward had finished her rhyming he struck his hands together, and said, 'It may be only an old bracelet, but when we get down there our fortunes are made.'

"And with that the tinkers whipped their horses and were away with the wind."

Kathleen was very downcast. "Conor here found that very bracelet in a lake near his home. But the Tinker Chief tricked him. We were following them to the fair to try to recover it."

Conor sighed. The great white road went north and the little roads went over the hills and far away, south, east and west, and who knew which one the tinkers had taken. "We'd best go home, Kathleen, and not be wasting our time."

The rosy woman laughed and put an arm around each of the children. "That's no talk now, and your adventures only starting. Wait now and we'll have a bit of dinner. It will put the heart into you and give you courage to continue your search."

Conor lit the stove and soon the rosy woman had a meal of meat-balls, potatoes and peas all ready. When the plates were empty she took an apple cake out of a tin, and sprinkled it with sugar while Kathleen made tea. The sun was still warm and on a nearby tree a little bird sang a few notes before he flew away.

While Kathleen washed and dried the dishes, Conor tried

to whistle the notes the bird had sung. They weren't quite right, so he took out his harmonica and began a tune he had never before played. The rosy woman had been dozing quietly, but at the sound of the music she opened her eyes and sat up.

"That's a grand tune, Conor. Long ago I heard it in the village of Ballingeary in the County of Cork. An old blind fiddler in the house above the bridge used to play it. Were you ever in Ballingeary?"

Conor put down his harmonica. "I wasn't then, ma'am, and the tune just came to me now. I've never before been away from home."

Kathleen emptied the tin basin into the field, and stored away the dishes. She rolled down her sleeves and came over. "I know the place well. Twice the tinkers camped there, near the Pass of Keimaneigh—over towards the lake of Gougane Barra."

The rosy woman rocked to and fro. "A beautiful place Gougane. Sometime I must go back there. Did you ever read the lovely poem written about it:

> "There is a green island in lone Gougane Barra
> Where allua of songs rushes forth as an arrow
> In deep-valley'd Desmond a thousand wild fountains
> Come down to that lake from their home in the mountains
> There grows the wild ash and the time-stricken willow"

Kathleen interrupted her. "Wait a minute."

"What is it?" The rosy woman was put out.

"The rhyme old Mary Ward had," Kathleen's voice was shrill with excitement. "Where the wild ash grows and the tawny brake. Where the mountains rise o'er the silver lake."

"The words fit. It could be describing Gougane Barra," agreed the Rosy Woman.

Kathleen pulled Conor to his feet and shook him in excitement. "Will we chance it? Will we go down to Gougane Barra in west Cork?"

"It's miles and miles away," Conor was hesitant. "But still if you say so, we'll go."

The rosy woman began to put away her pots and pans. "I'd like to take you down there, but I must go to Dublin city to buy silks and satins to sell all over Ireland. It's my living."

Kathleen helped her stack the things. "Of course we understand, ma'am. You have been very kind to us. We'll remember you."

Bran drove the horse back from the field where it was cropping, and stood on guard while the children yoked the caravan. Kathleen spoke softly to the black horse and he whinnied when he felt her hand on his neck.

The rosy woman climbed up on her seat and shook the reins. "Maybe we'll meet again. I hope we do. If ever you need a home, Kathleen, come to me and I'll take you in style travelling the roads of Ireland."

"Thank you, ma'am. It's a grand offer."

The rosy woman leaned down. "If you happen to meet my sister, Huckster Peg, tell her you're a friend of mine and she'll help you."

The caravan was moving away. "How will we know her?" shouted Conor.

"There are five stone steps down to her shop and the door has a tinkling bell, you can't miss it. Good-bye and luck be on your road."

Then the rosy woman turned the black horse over the wooden bridge and towards the faraway city of Dublin and Conor and Kathleen with Bran at their heels took the road to Gougane Barra in the deep south.

CHAPTER FIVE

THE ROAD TO THE PAST

The road south was easy underfoot. It led through the great bog of Allen, and here and there little mounds of turf were drying-out under the pale sun. Far away on the bog a man was piling a cart with oblong sods, and he waved to the children and they gaily waved back. They picked late blackberries on a stunted bush, and later gathered golden hazel nuts from a nut-grove a little way off the road. As they went along Kathleen told Conor the story of Aengus, Prince of the De Dannan.

"The De Dannans were fairy people who lived in Ireland thousands of years ago," she began. "Then one day great white ships out of Spain came sailing across the sea. The sailors were called Celts, and they had come to conquer Ireland. Twice the De Dannans raised up a magic mist and twice the ships floundered and almost sank. But at the third attempt the Celts beached their boats and drove the fairy people high into the Sliabh Mish Mountains. There the fairy people were defeated. Silently they crept into the heart of the mountains, for they could not bear to be driven away from Ireland.

"They had strange powers, but Aengus was the greatest magician of them all," continued Kathleen. "Sooner than go into the mountains and leave the sight of the hills, the spray of the waves and the sound of the wind forever behind, Aengus changed himself into a stag and roamed the great forests with the herd."

"And what happened then," Conor asked, while Bran moved forward with ears cocked to hear the story.

"When he was old, Aengus changed himself into a hawk, and for a long time he made his home on Mount Brandon.

When his life as a hawk was over he changed himself into a wolfhound, and then into a great red fox and then into a salmon.

"The story goes," continued Kathleen, "that when the salmon was very wise, Aengus resumed his own shape as Prince of the De Dannan, and went into the hills to his own people. And though ages had passed they recognised him at once, for his eyes were odd—one blue and one brown, and on his wrist he wore the royal bracelet of the Sidhe—all gold and carved."

"Maybe that was the bracelet I found," said Conor. "Maybe we'll meet Aengus and he'll help us outwit the Tinker Chief."

Overhead the grey clouds of evening were piling up. The wind had risen, and the curlews on the now distant bog wheeled and gave their lonely, long-lost cry.

The hills had fallen away sharply, and now the road was becoming more of a boreen than anything else. It meandered along in a hopeless fashion through the barren, bleak countryside. Here and there a solitary tree waved a skinny arm, and in the short November dusk took on the shape of a withered witch. Kathleen shivered. It seemed ages since they had seen house or habitation. Even the animals seemed to be asleep—all except poor Bran who trotted along whimpering to himself.

Kathleen looked at the grey twisting road, at the dark gathering clouds overhead. She saw something and her eyes brightened. "Look, Conor. Look, the first star out. Let's make a wish."

Together they chanted:

> "Star light, star bright, star shining in the night
> I wish I may, I wish I might, get the wish I wish
> tonight."

Around the bend the road forked into three. Just at the fork was a huge rock. "It's almost like a sign-post," said Conor.

"Or a stone man." Kathleen stood on her toes to look at it. "Remember the advice the little man in the mist gave us?"

"When you come to the place where three roads meet
Ask the stone man to direct your feet."

"It seems a silly thing to do." Conor was annoyed that he hadn't remembered the leprechaun's advice first.

"Oh well, I'll ask," said Kathleen. She looked up and said clearly. "Please, Mr. Stone Man, tell us the road to take."

As she said the words the moon came out and very clearly they saw the sign-post had directions. They said: "The Road to the Present; The Road to the Past; The Road to the Future."

Mystified the children stood and looked. There was a rumble like a peal of thunder and they heard the Stone Man speak:

"Three roads before you now you see
The past, the present, and what's to be
So make your choice, be brave, be bold
The stars are dimming, the night grows cold."

Kathleen stood rooted to the spot, but the dog had gone racing down one of the roads. "Come along," urged Conor. "Hurry or we'll lose Bran."

Kathleen still hesitated. "I'd like to take the Road to the Future. Wouldn't it be fun to see what's going to happen?"

The wind was gathering force, and now the sign-post was caught in a gale and spun crazily round and round. The moon went behind the clouds and for a moment the children stood at the cross-roads in utter darkness. The sign-post had steadied itself, but when the children looked they saw it was blank. And as for three roads. Well, under the moonlight all roads look alike.

"You wouldn't make up your mind in time," shouted Conor. "Now Bran is gone and we don't know which road to take."

Kathleen shrugged her shoulders. "We can't stand here all night. Let's take the centre road, and hope for the best."

Conor couldn't think of an answer, so sulkily he followed Kathleen. It was a queer, unreal journey they made. The moon was shining brightly, but she threw no shadows, and though the children walked briskly their footsteps made no sound at all. Over to their right a pin-point of light sparkled, was gone, and then shone more brightly again. The sky had a strange glow, and though there was no sound Kathleen felt that behind the trees was movement and life.

The path twisted and turned and ended abruptly against a clump of bushes. Beyond that was a clearing. Kathleen and Conor crouched down behind the bushes and watched. They saw a fire burning brightly and around it a band of tinkers. One figure detached himself from the group and for a moment stood outlined against the firelight. It was the tinker chief, dark and handsome. Around his neck was a yellow handkerchief and on his arm the gold bracelet. He came towards the bushes and Conor jumped. Kathleen could see nothing now for the moon had gone behind the clouds, but she could hear panting and scuffling.

The the moon broke free from the scudding clouds and Kathleen saw Conor lying on the ground, his arms around an old thorn bush. But there was neither sign nor light of the tinkers. Even the fire had disappeared, leaving not even a trace of ash behind.

Conor got to his feet, brushing the dead leaves from his coat. "What happened? I thought I had the tinker chief and then he vanished. What road are we on at all?"

"It can't be the road to the present. We haven't caught up with the tinkers yet."

"But we will," Kathleen was already running back to the cross-roads and Conor was hard put to catch up on her. "I've just remembered, there's a glen outside Ballingeary. A place ringed round with fairy thorns. The place we've seen could be that glen."

In a panic she caught Conor's arm. "We're on the Road to the Future. We must hurry back to the present before it's too late."

CHAPTER SIX

THE HOSTING OF THE SIDHE

When the children got back to the cross-roads the sign-post was blank and the place deserted. In the moonlight the Stone Man looked half alive, but he never spoke a word. Conor whistled and Kathleen called, "Bran. Where are you?" But there was no sign of the dog. Overhead great black clouds like witches on broomsticks chased each other across the sky, and the wind howled and moaned in the trees. Kathleen and Conor caught hands and with one accord went running down another road.

"I hope we're going the right way," Kathleen's voice was wobbly and her heart was thumping with fright.

"If only Bran were here he'd know. I only hope he isn't lost."

Something brushed past them. It was a tall man with a green cloak flying out behind him. By his side trotted a dog.

"Bran, come back," called Conor, but the dog didn't even turn his head.

The road wound and curved and they were hard set to keep the mysterious figure in sight. Sometimes the man and dog seemed to merge into the rocks, then they seemed to be nothing more than the shadows of a tree.

The ground was uneven. Kathleen stumbled over a stone and went sprawling against a bush. Conor fell on top of her. When they got to their feet they saw that the bush was taking on the shape of a cottage and light was breaking through a crack in the door.

"Knock on the door," whispered Kathleen, but before Conor could do as he was bid, the door opened and a girl with a pale, pointed face and long red hair beckoned them in.

A strange company was gathered in the room. People with

long flowing hair and dreamy eyes, dressed in cloaks and knee breeches and long sweeping gowns. The clothes were the colour of green grass, brown bogwater and scarlet fuchsia.

The man in the green cloak who had passed them on the road led them to a seat beside the fire, and a girl with red hair stood up and began to sing:

"Tonight's the hosting of the sidhe,
 Come away. Come away.
To the hollow hills and the glens where we
 Fly away. Fly away.

Where the moon rides high in the midnight sky,
 Far away. Far away.
By the breeze upblown on the clouds we'll fly
 Come away. Come away.

We'll swing on the stars in the silver light
And we'll sing and we'll dance through the livelong night
To the wild gay revels join hand in hand
With the fairy host come to fairyland,
 Come away. Come away."

From a nail beside the fire the fiddler took down his instrument and began to play. As he played the children were caught up in the dance. Ever afterwards they were to remember that night. Like leaves they were spun around. The room seemed to grow bigger until it was a great cavern. The fire grew so bright that it was hard to tell if it was fire or sun or moon that was shining. Shafts of light passed overhead and far away great bright stars hung out of a timeless sky. Kathleen, Conor, the dog, the host of the Sidhe were all caught up and carried over the hill-tops to the place where stars walk. And the stars and the company went whirling around in a mad, joyous dance of youth.

Then it was all over and the children were once more sitting by the fire while an old man told them a story.

"Once, long ago, the Princess Fionnula and her three brothers were enchanted by their wicked stepmother into the shape of swans. The swan-children were bound by the spell of the witch to spend three hundred years on Swan Lake, three hundred years on the stormy Sea of Moyle, and three hundred years on the wild Atlantic ocean."

The storyteller paused and the man in the green cloak smiled at Kathleen. Then she knew he was Aengus because his eyes were odd—one was blue and one was brown.

"Every year on November Eve, the swan children were disenchanted for the space of one hour," the storyteller went on. "One November Eve the host of fairyland came riding by on white horses. Aengus the Prince stopped to dance with Fionnula, and before he left he gave her the gold bracelet he wore on his arm. He told her to keep it to remember him by and that when the years of her enchantment were over he would return and take her and her brothers to fairyland."

"She lost the bracelet," whispered Kathleen, but the storyteller was speaking again.

"For seven years the swan-maiden kept the bracelet. Then it was time for her to leave Swan Lake and fly with her brothers to the Sea of Moyle. But her wicked stepmother put a spell of forgetfulness on her, and she left the bracelet behind her in the lake. Then in the twilight hour, and still in her swan shape she flew with her brothers over the mountains. She was never seen again, nor was the bracelet ever found."

Conor jumped excitedly to his feet. "It was. My dog found the bracelet in the lake. Now the Tinker Chief has it."

"Recover it. Recover it before it is too late," shouted the fairy company.

Far away a cock began to crow. The man in the green cloak held up his arm and Kathleen could see a white band against the brown where he had worn the bracelet.

"The dawn breaks. Our revels are ended. Come away. Come away."

And with a loud laugh the host of the Sidhe were caught up and swept out of the room.

The children followed them. Outside the dawn was breaking. The cottage was a whitethorn bush and beside it slept the little dog. Kathleen rubbed his head and he opened his eyes, jumped to his feet and with a bark that said quite plainly, "Follow me!" he went running down the road that unwound itself before them. Swinging, hand in hand, Conor and Kathleen followed after.

CHAPTER SEVEN

THE BALLAD SINGER

It was a bright, soft morning as the children walked along the high road to the south. They felt light and airy and soon they were chasing the little dog, and pretending to catch him. He ran between the legs of a grey-bearded man who was on the road before them. The man was swinging along, singing to himself. There were holes in his boots and his clothes were dusty and green with age, but his pockets were bulging with broadsheets—green, yellow, red and blue. His face was kind and his eyes twinkled, though he greeted the children in rather a stern voice.

"Is it miching from school you are, out on the roads at this hour of the day?"

"We're going to Gougane Barra. On business we are," explained Kathleen carefully. Conor only scowled.

"What signifies school when you have important matters on hand," said the Ballad Singer cheerfully. He winked an eye at Bran, and Kathleen could have sworn that the dog winked back.

"My name is Maurice," continued the stranger, rubbing his hand along his chin. "A ballad singer I am, and, though I say it myself, the best one travelling the roads today. What names would be on the three of you?"

"I'm Conor. This girl is Kathleen, and this is my dog Bran." Thoughtfully Conor eyed the bulging sheets in the man's pockets. "Are they ballads?"

"They are indeed." Maurice took out a bundle. "The green ones are threepence. A fair enough class of a ballad. The red ones are sixpence. Grand songs they are, some of them with twenty-seven verses."

"And the yellow ones. How much are they?" asked Kathleen, eyeing them curiously.

"Arra, they're only a penny each. Ones the whole country-side would be singing, like *A Jug of Punch*." To listen to the tone of Maurice's voice you'd realise that he had little respect for the yellow sheets. Thoughtfully he cleared his throat and hummed a few bars. "I sell them at fairs and market-towns," he said a trifle boastfully, "and as long as the voice holds out I'll never want."

"It's well for you," Kathleen was envious. "I never had more than sixpence in my whole life."

"Do you sing at all?" Maurice asked her.

"A little."

"I play the harmonica," put in Conor anxiously. It wasn't often he spoke to strangers of his talent, but he wanted to earn the respect of the Ballad Singer who seemed so sure of himself, despite his rags.

The Ballad Singer looked pleased. "Play a few bars and I'll sing a song," he suggested. " 'Twill pass the time." And with that he struck up *The Irish Rover.*

"We had one million bags of the best Sligo rags
We had two million barrels of bone
We had three million bales of old nanny goats' tails
We had four million barrels of stone.
We had five million hogs and six million dogs,
And seven million barrels of porter.
We had eight million sides of blind horses' hides.
In the hold of the Irish Rover."

The children started to laugh—but Bran trotted away in disgust for the last verse:

"We had sailed seven years when the measles broke out
And the ship lost her way in a fog.
And the whole of the crew was reduced unto two
'Twas meself and the Captain's old dog.
Then the ship struck a rock, oh lord what a shock
And nearly tumbled over
Turned nine times around, and the poor dog was drowned.
'Twas the last of the Irish Rover."

When they had finished Conor put his harmonica back in his pocket and sighed, "I can't play any more. I'm too hungry."

"I could do with some breakfast meself, not to speak of

Kathleen and Bran here," agreed Maurice equably. "And here we are at the very place where we'll get some, and a welcome too."

Confidently he turned into a small passage that led through an undergrowth. Hesitantly the children and dog followed him. The trees, looping overhead, shut out the sun, and for a little while they walked through the gloomy cavern in silence. Then the path widened and brightened, and finally led them to a grassy clearing, in the centre of which stood a little house, shaped exactly like a horseshoe.

"Horseshoe House," said Kathleen, half to herself.

"The very thing," agreed Maurice, "and a grand, lucky place it is to visit." He gave a peculiar whistle and immediately a window upstairs opened; a head with a brown cap with red tassels bobbed out, and a thin, reedy voice piped:

"Is that yourself, Maurice? Hold hard a minute. Loo will be down to let you in."

Almost immediately the door opened and a little man wearing an almost identical cap, but with green tassels bobbing out of it, stood on the threshold. His little face stretched wide with a smile. He reminded Kathleen of the heads they carved out of turnips at Hallowe'en.

"This is my good friend, Loo the Leprechaun," explained Maurice. He pushed the children forward. "This is Kathleen, and this is Conor, and they have their dog Bran with them." He looked around, but the dog had vanished.

"Never mind," piped Loo, "he'll come back. They always do."

Kathleen wondered who the mysterious 'they' were. Then, as if reading her thoughts, Loo added, "He'll come when the Cat comes." And without more ado, he led them down a narrow hall and into a wide kitchen at the back of the house. The little man who had called out by the window was rushing around setting the table, and now and again giving a stir to a big pot that sent out a grand, warm, satisfying smell. Conor sniffed. Then he sat down on the edge of the chair, almost weak with hunger.

"This is the brother, Beg," said Loo, grandly waving towards the cook. "He's the second cleverest Leprechaun in the world. I'm the cleverest."

At this statement, Beg looked sulky, but before he could dispute this point, Maurice put in easily, "Where is Báinín?"

"Gone to Kilkenny to help crown the King of the Cats," said Loo a trifle mournfully. He sat down beside Maurice, making absolutely no attempt to help his busy little brother. "You didn't meet her on the roads?" he asked.

Maurice smiled. "I did not then. I met a purple cow, a dog with a squint, a white blackbird and a galloping snail, but never a sign or light of a white cat.

The little man sighed at this, but said nothing. Conor was impatiently watching the preparation of the breakfast, but Kathleen was more interested in the kitchen. She thought it was the loveliest place she had ever been in. The windows were shaped like horseshoes, and the bench on which they were sitting had horses' heads carved on the back and sides. Pictures of fairy men and women, riding the white horses of fairyland, were pinned on the walls, and even the bellows hanging from a nail by the fire was in the shape of a bridle.

Beg ladled the steaming porridge into blue and white bowls, and, while Loo helped them to sugar and cream, he fried a panful of eggs and bacon and wet a pot of tea. It wasn't until they were all fed that he sat down himself.

"Talking of Báinín," he began, but he didn't get any further. Something long and white and silky came sailing gracefully through the open window, followed by a clumsy, brown ball. It was Báinín and Bran. The cat looked at Beg disdainfully.

"And what about me?" she said haughtily.

Maurice began to laugh, and Beg looked guilty, but the children were open-mouthed with astonishment.

"The . . . . . . the cat can talk," stuttered Conor.

Báinín looked down her nose. "So can you, but *I* don't remark on it. Besides, I am the cleverest and most famous cat in all Ireland."

"And 'tis yourself that knows it," chuckled Maurice.

Báinín's eyes turned green, the way they did when she spied a mouse. "Is this my dear friend, Maurice the Ballad Singer, I see," she purred. "Dear, dear, if you hadn't spoken I should never have recognised you. You grow odder looking every time I meet you." Her voice grew even more sarcastic, "And how is the voice holding out?"

"Fair enough, no complaints as yet," said Maurice cheerfully. He bent down to stroke Báinín's back, but, with a flick of her well-kept tail, she leaped out of his reach and onto a small stool. There she sat, gazing steadily into the fire, while Bran sat at her feet, his eyes fixed on her in honest admiration. Conor couldn't credit his eyesight—his dog, who normally couldn't abide cats.

CHAPTER EIGHT

THE TINKER AGAIN

When the children had helped Beg to clear up the breakfast things and sweep the kitchen, Maurice rose to go. The Leprechaun, meanwhile, had been recounting in a loud voice, the saga of his travels. In all the adventures that befell him—according to himself—he was the hero of the story. Báinín accompanied him on most of his journeyings, but Beg stayed at home and kept the house clean, cooked the meals, milked the cows, and fed the chickens and pigs. Kathleen was sorry for Beg, but the little man had such a vast admiration for his brother that her sympathy was wasted.

The grandfather clock tick-tocked and then boomed out twelve. The sun, high in the heavens, slanted through the homespun curtains. Maurice crammed his battered hat on the back of his head and felt for his pipe. "Thanks for the grand breakfast," he said, "but now I'm afraid we must be on our way."

The two little men filled their pipes from Maurice's tin box. "Where are you off to now?"

"I'm for the Fair of Bantry, and the children . . ."

"The children are following the Tinker Tribe," said the White Cat without removing her gaze from the fire.

There was a small silence, then Bran gave an apologetic bark and Kathleen said quickly, "We're going in search of a gold . . . . ."—but she got not further. There was a rustle of confusion and a clicking of tongues and the two little men vanished through the door.

"I should have warned you," said Maurice sadly. "At the mention of gold they're off."

"Where?" asked Kathleen, her eyes round with amazement.

The White Cat dropped down from her perch on the stool, and arched her back. "To see if their crocks are safe and sound." She yawned, covering her mouth with a delicate paw. "I wouldn't be a leprechaun for all the gold in Tara. It's not worth the trouble." She looked disdainfully in Kathleen's direction, "but as you were saying when our friends took off, you're in search of a gold . . . .?"

"A gold bracelet," explained Kathleen humbly. "The Tinker Chief found it. But it belongs to Conor."

"I suspected as much," said the White Cat darkly, "on my way home from Kilkenny I passed them on the road. I knew something was up. I went over to hear what it was all about, but the Tinker Chief pushed me away." She sniffed, "I gave him something to remember me by."

"Where are they now?" asked Maurice, putting his pipe in his pocket.

"Not a stone's throw away from here," said the White Cat grandly. "Follow me and I'll lead you to them. It's time you recovered your property."

Conor felt nervous of confronting the tinkers, just like that, but the Cat was not a person to trifle with. They followed her out of the house, through a field of mushrooms and then down to the river. Across the way was the tinker encampment.

"This is where we cross," explained the Cat. Without more ado, Bran plunged obediently in and began to swim across. The Cat twitched her whiskers in amused tolerance. "Dogs are such impulsive creatures."

"There doesn't seem to be any other way to cross," began Kathleen, but the Cat was leaping onto what at first appeared to be a pebble. As her paws touched it, it widened out into a flat stone. She leaped again, and the second pebble was now also flat. By the time she reached the far bank, seven white stones spanned the river, making an easy passage.

On the far side the cat lead them along the bank. She walked noiselessly along, and they followed on tiptoes. Then it happened. Kathleen stumbled over a trailing vine that hid the root of a tree. She had stumbled once before on the Road to the Past, and now her ankle twisted and she cried out in pain.

"Be careful," barked Bran, but no one knew what he meant, and the tinker dogs in the encampment barked in answer " It's too late."

The White Cat vanished up a tree, while Conor and Maurice tried to drag Kathleen to her feet, but the tinkers were surrounding them, and there was no escape.

"By the powers that be," shouted the Tinker Chief, "if it isn't our wandering Kathleen. And she's brought her friends with her."

One of the tribe poked Maurice in the ribs. "It's the Ballad Singer we met in Galway town."

The Tinker Chief was in good humour. "We'll have music and dancing tonight, and the very night for it too."

He lifted Kathleen to her feet and carried her to a yellow caravan, while a band of tinkers frog-marched Conor and the Ballad Singer along behind. They pushed them into a yellow caravan and locked the door on the outside. Then they went away laughing and pushing each other.

Conor looked glumly around. "Why didn't you make a run for it, Maurice? You could have got away."

Maurice pushed his hat back on his head and sat down beside Kathleen. " Arra I might as well spend a night here as any place." He loosened Kathleen's shoe and ran his strong, brown fingers gently over her ankle. " Does it hurt much?"

"Hardly anything," said Kathleen bravely, though tears were in her eyes, and she felt as if red-hot needles were stabbing her foot.

Conor stood on a box and peered through the curtained windows. "There's something up," he announced. "Lots of caravans are arriving and there's great comings and goings out there."

Kathleen tried to get up to look out, but had to sit down suddenly. When she got back her breath, she said, "I've just remembered. It's the gathering of the tribes to elect the King of all the Tinkers. Maybe they'll elect the Tinker Chief."

For a little while no one said anything, for they were all

hungry and dispirited. The evening was falling fast, throwing the caravan into half-shadows. Now and again Conor whistled at the window, but Bran had vanished. Maurice sat smoking while Kathleen closed her eyes and tried to remember Conor's grandmother and the cosy cottage at the foot of the mountains. She hoped the old woman wasn't worrying too much. If it hadn't been for the pain in her ankle she would have fallen asleep, for it had been a long day.

So bemused were they that the door opened and a ragged tinker boy was standing inside before they realised it. He put his hands on his hips and grinned.

"The Tinker Chief sent for ye all. He's to be crowned King of the Tinkers tonight. The Ballad Singer is to sing his 'come allyees', the boy is to give a rendering on his harmonica, and Kathleen is to dance. Entertainers all." He doubled over with laughter.

Conor shook his fist under the tinker's nose. "If you lay a finger on Kathleen, I'll flatten you."

"You and how many more?" jeered the boy, but Maurice was lifting Kathleen up.

"Have sense, Conor," he said reasonably. "If the Tinker Chief sent for us, we'll have to go."

The tinkers were gathering around an immense fire, laughing and shouting. As the Ballad Singer carried Kathleen over, the Chief detached himself from the group and came to meet them. Tonight he looked a queer wild figure. He wore a scarlet velvet coat and a green sash around his waist. He looked like a pirate chief, with a red handerchief tied around his long, black hair and big gold ear-rings swung from his ears. On his arm was the gold bracelet. His voice, when he spoke, was loud and arrogant.

"Look at me. I'm to be the Tinker King," he boasted and then burst into his rallying song:

"Oh I am the King of the Tinkers bold
And I walk with a ring of silver and gold.
I travel the roads with a careless swagger
Afraid of no man, king or beggar."

And with a shout the whole tribe joined in.

> "Yes, he's the King of the Tinkers bold
> And he walks with a ring of silver and gold."

The Chief was well away now. Loudly he continued.

> "With plenty of horses and caravans bright,
> On the roads by day, in the fields by night,
> For years I've searched for a bracelet old:
> Now I know the secret of fairy gold.
>
> "My people are wanderers—that's our breed—
> Of old Irish stock and of Irish creed.
> So lift your glasses, let all of ye sing,
> Ere the night passes, 'tis I will be King."

There was a great roar from the tribe as they all took up the chant:

> "Yes, he'll be King of the Tinkers bold
> And at every fair will his deeds be told."

They were all laughing and shouting. Old women were waving tin mugs; the younger ones were dancing, while children and dogs ran under foot. The Chief, amid a cheer, suddenly leaped over the fire. Behind the trees Bran waited and bided his time. Then, like a streak of lightning he was sailing through the air. He landed between the Chief's legs—and the Chief fell over. The tinker dogs rushed in and now the place was a bedlam of snapping dogs, shouting children and tinkers all mixed up on the ground.

Quickly the Ballad Singer lifted Kathleen up on his shoulder and walked swiftly away from the tinker camp.

CHAPTER NINE

HUCKSTER PEG

The Ballad Singer swung down the road with Conor beside him. Kathleen, seated on his shoulder, looked back. Bright flame fingers from the tinker fire were licking the sky, but the noise of the camp was growing fainter with every step they took. Bran came galloping after them, his tail like a mast at full-sail.

"You're a grand old dog," praised Conor, "you saved us." Bran ran around in little circles, pleased with himself. "Do you think maybe they'll follow us?" he asked Kathleen.

"Not tonight. The Chief daren't leave the camp for fear someone else would be elected in his stead. Seven times he's tried to have himself crowned, but each time some of the more powerful tinkers from the South have beaten him."

"Beaten him? How?" The ways of the tinkers were strange to Conor.

"Oh he'll have to wrestle, sing the loudest, tell the most stories and show as much gold as the next, or maybe more. I'd say the gold bracelet would weigh heavily in his favour—it being fairy gold."

From far away came a cry, followed by hilarious laughter. Then silence.

"I wonder will we ever get the bracelet back," puzzled Conor, "now we're running away from the tinkers. Maybe we'd better go home."

Maurice shifted Kathleen onto his left shoulder and paused. "From what you told me of the story, and what you saw on the Road to the Future, I'd say your best plan would be to go to Gougane Barra in the County of Cork. Wasn't that where you were making for? If the thing is ever to be solved, it will happen there. My advice is to avoid the tinkers until you all meet in Gougane."

"Anyhow," put in Kathleen, "we can't go home now. What about Aengus and the Swan Children? They're depending on us."

"And they'll help you, never fear."

The night had become very dark. Conor and Bran were trotting along, but the measured thread of the Ballad Singer never altered its rhythm.

They passed through a hamlet, but all the doors were shut, and everyone seemed to be in bed. They went over a bridge and into a little valley. A small huckster shop stood a little off the path. Light gleamed in the diamond-shaped windows, and the children could see an assortment of sweets and peggy's legs, and tins of meat, fruit and milk all jumbled together. Behind the counter was a woman with dark hair and gold ear-rings in her ears.

The Ballad Singer pushed in the door. A bell tinkled cheerfully, and by the time they had descended the five stone steps, the woman was out from behind the counter to greet them. She was singing to herself, and Kathleen thought the words of the song suited her. It was an old ballad and went like this:

> "As I walked down to Galway city
> At the hour of twelve of the night
> Who should I see but the Spanish lady
> Combing her hair by candlelight."

Spanish combs held the woman's coils of hair in place, and her eyes were as dark as those of any lady out of Spain.

She threw up her hands when she saw her visitors, and her voice was warm and welcoming. "Why if it isn't Maurice, the Ballad Singer. You're welcome."

The Ballad Singer put Kathleen sitting on the counter and mopped his face with a red handkerchief. "I hope you'll extend the welcome to my two young friends here. They're on their way to Gougane Barra." And he told her all about the Swan Children and the gold bracelet, and how the Chief wanted to become King of the Tinkers.

"It will all come out right in the end, never fear," said the woman. She caught Kathleen up and carried her into the comfort of the kitchen. "I'm called Huckster Peg. What names are on the two of you?"

"I'm Conor and this is Kathleen, and this is our dog Bran."

"I recognised the shop when we came in," said Kathleen. "A bell that rings and five steps down to the shop. We met your sister—a rosy woman in a caravan. She was on her way to Dublin city. She said you would help us, if we met you."

"And why wouldn't I," smiled Huckster Peg. She stirred a pot of soup on the fire, and then gave them each a bowlful. She gave Bran a dish of bread and soup, with thick pieces of meat through it.

"I know the Tinker Chief," she said, "and I know why he is so anxious to keep the bracelet. There's a legend that one day a gold bracelet would be found in the Swan Lake and that everyone who handled it would get his or her wish. That's why the Tinker Chief is so anxious to keep it. He wants to become King."

"But I'll have to get it back," thought Conor, or the Swan Children will never be disenchanted.

The children had mugs of cocoa and slices of bread and jam, and the Ballad Singer had a pot of strong tea and a ham sandwich. When they had finished, the Ballad Singer pushed back his chair, lit his pipe with a red turf and put his battered hat on the back of his head. "I never yet spent two nights running under the roof of a house, so if you'll promise to nurse Kathleen until her ankle is better, I'll be off."

Conor's face fell at the news, and Bran gave a plaintive bark. Kathleen hastily brushed away a tear; but, having spent many a long year with the tinkers, she understood that a house, however cosy, can stifle a person used to the sea-roads and the river-roads, and the stars and the sky for company.

The little dog picked up the Ballad Singer's blackthorn

stick and carried it in his mouth to the door, with Conor beside him. Even Kathleen insisted on hobbling out to wave 'good-bye'.

The wind whistled past and caught up a handful of dead leaves in play; the clouds drifted heedlessly by; the night was very silent, for the tinkers were far away, and the valley was hushed. "Won't you be lonely?" asked Conor in a lost voice.

The Ballad Singer laughed. "Not a bit of it. Night-time is the best for walking when you know the roads. It's a grand life going along without a care or bother and with no company but your own shadow!" He twirled his blackthorn gaily and smiled, "but I wouldn't advise it for young people like yourselves. The 'Good People' might run away with ye."

Kathleen tossed her head proudly. "We've met them twice since we started on our journey, and they only helped us to find the way. The little man in the mist told us what to ask the Stone Man, and the two little leprechauns and the White Cat were kind and good."

At this the Ballad Singer chuckled, "Ah, well, they like the young folk best of all, and why wouldn't they, for they are eternally young themselves." He paused a moment, his eyes on the distant stars. Then he buttoned up his coat and went swinging down the road, his pockets bulging with his blue and red and yellow broadsheets. The children and dog watched until he was out of sight; then, a little sadly, they went back into the warm kitchen.

Huckster Peg knew more about herbs and country cures than many, and before Kathleen went to bed, she bathed the sprain and rubbed it with a home-made ointment. Next morning, when Kathleen put her foot to the ground, her sprain was completely cured!

After breakfast, Huckster Peg cut up sandwiches, filled two bottles with milk, filled a bag with toffee and two rosy apples and put them all into a school satchel, which Conor slung over his shoulder. Then she took them outside the cottage to where a small, brown donkey was placidly nibbling a few thistles. He opened his mouth and 'hee-hawed' in the politest fashion. Kathleen gave him a piece of ginger bread which Huckster Peg had made, and he gobbled it up.

"Brownie is a great pet, aren't you, old fellow," and Huckster Peg rubbed the donkey's coat. Kathleen thought he was the best-cared-for animal she had ever seen.

"I'm going to lend him to you for your journey," explained Huckster Peg. "He'll take you to Gougane Barra and back. 'Tis a long journey and your ankle is still weak, alannah."

The donkey's ears dropped at this, and Conor asked, "Won't he be lonely?"

Huckster Peg shook her head. "He's a wise animal and knows what he knows. Just now you need him. 'Twould be best for Kathleen to ride him for a bit. Besides Bran will be company. Animals understand each other—just the way humans do."

Bran barked. Brownie knelt on his front legs and Kathleen climbed up on his back. Huckster Peg shook with laughter. "There now, didn't I tell you. Good-luck in your search, and if on the roads you happen to meet my sister Red Biddy, tell her you met me and she'll help you."

"How will we know her?" asked Kathleen.

"She wears a check apron. She's at every fair in the country, and she sells the strongest tea, the freshest sandwiches and the sweetest cake," smiled Huckster Peg.

She waved until they were out of sight, then went in muttering to herself. "Ah wisha God help them, the scraps. But I know Brownie will take good care of them and Bran is a clever wee dog. And Red Biddy will help them when she meets them."

And with that comforting thought she began to scrub the shelves and pile them high with coloured sweets in shining jars.

CHAPTER TEN

THE SWAN CHILDREN

The road, high, wide and white, stretched before the children. Away in the distance the mountains, blue and white-tipped, looked like giant ice-cream cones.

Kathleen had never enjoyed a ride more. The brown donkey lifted his hoofs high and trotted along, and neither Conor nor Bran had any trouble in keeping up with him.

Around the bend of the road was a bridge. At the sight of it the donkey stopped dead, but Bran raced excitedly over the bridge, then he turned tail and came at an even faster clip, back.

"Hee-haw," said the donkey, "I suspect trouble."

"The tinkers are over the bridge," barked Bran. "We had better hide."

Conor looked at Kathleen—"What on earth is the matter with the pair of them. I wish we could understand what they are saying to each other."

Kathleen climbed down, and Conor tried to lead the donkey forward, but he only dug in his heels and hee-hawed impatiently. Bran was tugging at Conor's trousers—"Come down under the bridge," he barked. "They won't see us there."

"Hee-haw," said the donkey. "Go on and I'll follow you. We're only wasting time."

The dog went galloping down the embankment with the donkey after him. They stopped just at the river's edge. Conor caught Kathleen's hand and began to run. "We'd better follow. I don't know what's up, but they're both scared."

They were just in time. A cart rumbled over the bridge and then another and another. The tinkers were on the move once more. They shouted and laughed and quarrelled, and the sharp eyes of the Tinker Chief seemed to see the very moss growing under the stones, but they missed out the children and animals crouching breathlessly below them.

"That was a narrow escape," said Conor when the tinkers had passed on. "We certainly don't want to meet the Chief again."

"We'll have to face him in Gougane Barra," sighed Kathleen, "but it's time enough then. The donkey was very clever."

"Bran was just as clever," said Conor, a little sharply. "He spotted the tinkers first. It's just as well that he and the donkey understand each other.

The noise of the carts died away. The dust settled down, and the sun that had been sulking all morning, decided to come out and see the world. The donkey hee-hawed gaily, kicking his heels, and was up and over the bridge with the children and dog following hard behind.

"We seem to be taking a different road to the tinkers," said Conor anxiously. "I hope the donkey knows his way."

Kathleen tossed her head. "He is probably taking a short cut. We'd best leave it to him."

At midday they stopped by a lonely lake to have their lunch. They ate the sandwiches, cake and milk that Huckster Peg had packed, and then had an apple each. They gave Bran a meaty bone which was in the satchel, and the brown donkey a bunch of carrots and a few lumps of sugar. Four white swans came gliding across the lake and paused by the bank while the children fed them with the remains of the food.

When they had finished, Kathleen lay back to enjoy the sunshine and Conor took out his harmonica and began to play. The donkey kicked up his heels and trotted around to the music. A hare came looping out of a field and two brown and white rabbits. They jumped and began to play leap-frog over the dog's back. Conor rubbed his eyes to make sure he wasn't dreaming. Never before had he seen the like.

The water of the lake stirred in the wind and a few drops of rain fell on his nose. Reluctantly he put his harmonica in his pocket and stood up. The hare and the rabbit scampered away, and Kathleen got up on the donkey's back and leaned down to pull Conor up. Then the donkey went galloping away, with Bran racing to keep up with him.

The four white swans rose out of the lake and went flying before them. The sky was darkening, and the countryside around was solitary and bleak, broken only by the outlines of a gaunt castle.

"We'd best take shelter," said Kathleen. She wondered was the place empty and dug her heels into the donkey's side to drive him towards it. He seemed reluctant to go.

The children went up to the castle doorway, and Bran whimpered with fright. Rain was pouring down on the donkey, but he wouldn't come nearer for shelter. An old woman came shuffling along a dark and dismal passage. "Come into the kitchen," she wheedled the children.

"Hee-haw," brayed the donkey. "Watch out, Bran. I don't

trust the old woman." But the dog had spotted a mouse and was gone chasing him into the castle.

The old woman led the children into a big stone kitchen which was dusty with age. A beady spider swung from its web on the ceiling and Bran was growling and chasing the mouse around the room. A big pot of soup was bubbling on an old-fashioned fire. The old woman put three broken dishes on a table and began to ladle out soup. The wind swept down the chimney and soot and sparks blew every-

where. One of the sparks stung the mouse and it ran up the old woman's cloak. Bran jumped up after him, and the pot of soup crashed to the floor.

Or was it soup? Clouds of vapour were rising, and the stench was terrible. The children choked and coughed, and the old woman screamed and raised her arms. And now the children saw that two terrible wings were rising out of her shoulder blades.

"Bad cess to that dog," she screamed, " he's broken my spell. I turned my silly step-daughter, the Princess Fionnula and her brothers into swans. I'll turn you all into pigs."

Bran turned tail and went flying out of the kitchen, and terror-stricken, the children fled after him. At the door they almost collided with the brown donkey. Somehow, they never knew how, they were up on his back and he was running away through the storm. Kathleen looked back, but now the castle was only a broken-down ruin, and a great black bird was rising in the sky over it.

Thunder rolled and lightning flashed and the brown donkey reared on his hind-legs with terror. Sheltering under a tree were the swans—only one was half-swan and half-girl, with long golden hair.

"Come and join us," called the girl, in a far-away voice. "We are the Swan Children. Come and shelter with us."

The donkey trotted over, and Conor and Kathleen went under the shelter of her feathery cloak.

"I know you," said Kathleen. "You are the Children of Lir."

"Enchanted by the jealousy of our stepmother, the Witch, to the shape of swans. She led us to the shores of the Lake and told us to bathe in the water."

"And there she turned you into four white swans," whispered Kathleen.

From a great distance a voice seemed to come, so that the children did not know if the Swan Girl was speaking, or if it was merely the whispering of the trees.

"Out from your home, be swans of Darvra's waves,
With clamorous birds begin your life of gloom.
Children shall weep your fate, but none can save
For I've pronounced the dreadful words of doom."

The Swan Girl was speaking again:

"Three hundred years we have spent on smooth Lake Darvra; three hundred years on the stormy Sea of Moyle, and three hundred years on Erris—the black and bitter waters."

"And will you never be disenchanted?" asked Kathleen sadly.

"When Aengus finds his gold bracelet, all will be well. But beware of the Witch. Beware of her spells." The eyes of the Swan Girl were bright with moonshine and her voice was

heavy with enchantment. "We are the greatest of the sorrows of storytelling. The tragic Children of Lir."

Conor rubbed his eyes. Four white swans were rising in the sky, but one dropped down a white feather. Kathleen stooped and picked it up, but it crumbled away in her hand and was nothing but dust.

The storm had spent itself. Silently the children climbed up on the back of the donkey, and he and the dog trotted away until the haunted place was far behind.

CHAPTER ELEVEN

THE LITTLE MEN OF THE BOG

In a little while they came to a fork in the road. In the moonlight one road was fine and wide, and the other, narrow and stony, seemed to lead towards a wilderness of mountain. This time Bran led the way and the brown donkey followed the dog up the mountain road.

It curved and twisted and in the end seemed to be leading nowhere in particular. For a long time Kathleen said nothing. Then she whispered to Conor, for she didn't wish to annoy the animals, "Do you think are we lost?"

Conor looked at the road that had narrowed itself to a goat track, and seemed to be bringing them to the edge of a great bog. It needed all his confidence in the dog and the donkey to make him answer. "I'm sure they know where they're going. They are more clever than we think."

Far away on the bog a pin-point of light moved, flickered, steadied itself and moved again. Kathleen caught hold of the donkey's ears in excitement and Bran began to run a little faster.

"Look, Conor," she said, "look! Light on the bog. What are they?"

Once more the lights danced. "Will o' the wisps," said Conor, peering into the gloom.

Kathleen's eyes were sharper. "No, they're little men. Hundreds of them. They're coming towards us, singing something. Listen."

The wind drifted by, bringing with it the perfume of the heather and the sounds of the bog:

"Oh we are the Keepers of the Bog,
We come in the mist and the sweeping fog.
With our lanterns bright we lead the way
To the weary traveller gone astray."

The sounds died away and then rose again in waves:

"For we are the Keepers of your Dreams,
You'll hear our song in the rushing streams;
If you follow its course, perhaps you'll find
You have lost your way, but never mind.

For we are the friends of the young in heart,
Tho' we've watched you from the very start,
It is here past the bogholes grim and stark
We must guide your steps through the fog and dark.

We are the Keepers of the Bog."

Then around the children were hundreds and hundreds of little men, dressed in russet, with faces like crab-apples in Autumn and eyes the colour of the brown bog pools. Each one carried a torch in his withered hand. Some of them scrambled up on the donkey's head. More got up behind Conor and still more got up on Bran's back. Then the remainder kept pace with the two animals as they sped delicately over the bog pools and morass to the far side of the brown expanse.

In the very middle of the bog a huge turf fire was blazing, and as the little men came up to it they threw their torches into the flames so that they now rose in the sky like a gigantic light. More little men were gathered around the fire, half sitting, half lying. When the brown donkey came up they clapped their hands and said:

"Welcome, brown donkey. Welcome, dog. Welcome, children. Come and join the fun."

The donkey bent his forelegs so that Kathleen slipped easily off his back and into the heather. Conor sat down beside her. The donkey kicked his heels and began to race around, while the little men took rides on the dog's back.

On the fire was a huge, three-legged cauldron. One little man ran around ladling out stew with a delicious smell, into tiny dishes. "They're too small," said Conor to himself in dismay. "We'll never get a bite." But when he looked down he had a big dish filled to the brim.

Then the little men passed around a jug and each took a drink and wiped the rim. Kathleen and Conor thought they had never tasted anything sweeter or more heart-warming. The little men called it mead, and drowsily Conor remembered that he had once heard from his grandmother of how, in the olden days, people brewed mead from the heather-honey, but now the secret was lost.

"Except with us," whispered a voice in his ear. The sound brought Conor back from his dreams to the purple bog and the little men around him.

One of them was standing on a little mound and the remainder were shouting, "A story. A story."

"One morning I was out before the dawn," began the little man, "and under a bridge by the river I met two children. One of them played a harmonica so sweetly and so tunefully that I placed him and the girl under the protection of the men of the bog."

More of the little men jumped to their feet and shouted, "Let the boy play so that we may judge for ourselves."

Conor stirred uneasily, "I'm scared to play, Kathleen. I'm not very good, and the little men mightn't like my music."

Kathleen gave his arm a friendly squeeze. "You'll be all right. If you pleased one, you'll please the lot."

Many a time afterwards, Kathleen tried to remember that night on the bog, but it was mixed up in her mind with fire-light, the scent of the heather and the bright picture of little men in green and brown with high boots and pointed hats. And now Conor was playing an old tune, *The Queen of Connemara,* and they were all rocking in time and singing:

"Oh my boat can safely float in the teeth of wind and weather,
And can race the fastest hooker between Galway and Kinsale;
When the black floor of the ocean and the white foam leap together,

High she rides in her pride, like a seagull thro' the gale.
Oh she's neat, oh she's sweet, she's a beauty every line,
The *Queen of Connemara* is that bounding bark of mine."

Far away a bird sang out, and another, and another, answered the dawn chorus. The sky was reddening, and a sudden gust of wind sprang up over the bog. Where the little men had been, there were now hundreds of leaves, brown, green and russet.

The brown donkey came trotting over the turf, and Bran was beside him, tail wagging hard with excitement. The donkey knelt down and Kathleen sprang up on his back.

"Would you like a ride too," she asked Conor. He laughed, "Indeed I would not. I'll race Bran instead."

They started to gallop—and lo and behold they were at the edge of the bog and a fine white road was stretching out before them.

CHAPTER TWELVE

THE ROAD TO THE FAIR

There were dozens of people on the road—men driving herds of fat bullocks; women driving cross looking geese; farmers, red-faced and burly, sitting on high carts loaded with cabbages, apples and sacks of potatoes. Bran edged in between a boy carrying turf and a small red-cheeked woman with a basket of eggs on her head. The brown donkey followed the dog.

"There's a woeful crowd going the roads this day," said the woman fretfully, "all off to the fair. Hard set I am to keep the eggs from crashing to the ground."

"This load of turf is so heavy, I'm worn out carrying it," grumbled the boy. Kathleen, fine and comfortable on the donkey's back, felt sorry for them.

"I'll get down and maybe the donkey will carry the turf and eggs a bit of the road for you."

Bran barked angrily at the suggestion of loading down his friend, but the donkey didn't seem to care. Delightedly the woman and the boy slung the eggs and the turf across his back. Kathleen marched proudly between them.

"You're a grand agreeable girl," said the woman, warmly. "I suppose you're going to the Bantry Butter Fair like the remainder of us?"

"We're making for Gougane Barra," said Kathleen. She looked around for Conor, but there was no sign of him. She tried to stand on her tip-toes, but a fat man pushed her in the back. Bran growled at this, but the fat man growled back. "Get along out of that, the lot of ye, or the cattle will run ye down. This is no place for dreaming."

The little, fat woman was chatting away. "So you're off to Gougane Barra. You have a good step before you, but still and all you'll have time at the fair for a meal and a bit of fun. When I sell the eggs and Dinny here sells the turf, I'll buy ye hot apple cakes and tea from Red Biddy at the stalls."

"We met her sisters," said Kathleen proudly. "One has a caravan and goes around Ireland selling silks and laces. Then there's Huckster Peg. She has a shop and the donkey belongs to her. She loaned him to us."

"Mind that now," the little woman was impressed. "You must travel around a lot."

The wind blew up, carrying snow before it. Conor was at the tail-end of the crowd going the road. Someone had

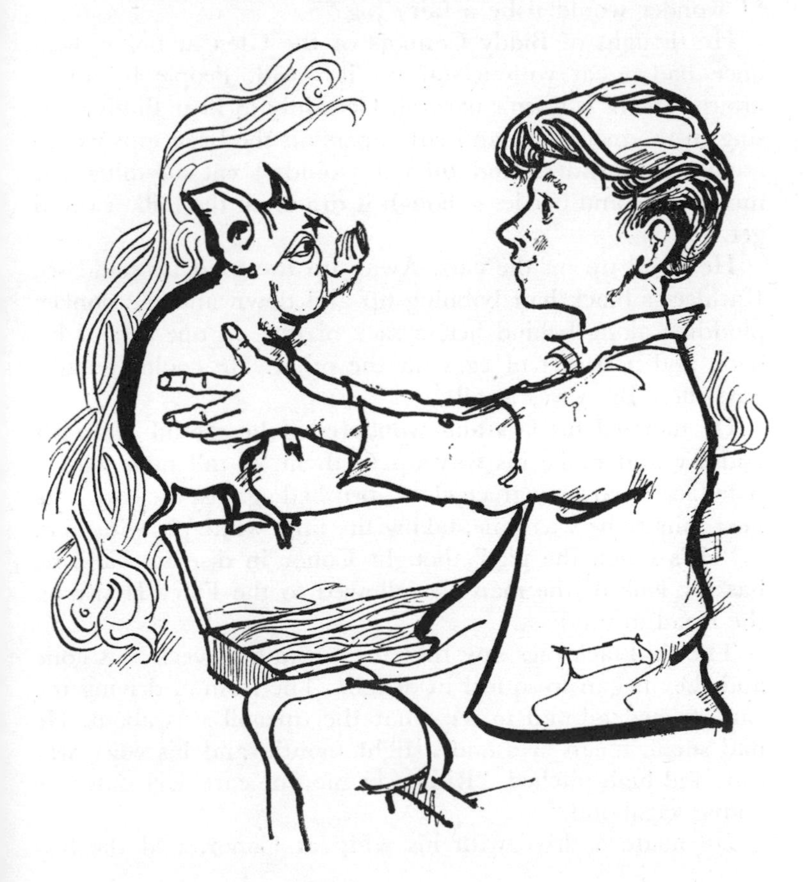

stood on the end of his boot-lace, and he fell. When he picked himself up and tied his boot tightly, there was no sign of Kathleen or the brown donkey. He ran along, but he couldn't squeeze in between a high, red cart and a flock of sheep.

"I might as well ride as walk," he said, and swung himself up on the tail of the cart.

Six black pigs and a tiny white bonaveen were huddled in a corner. The black pigs grunted and squealed and made little bites at their wee white brother.

"The runt of the litter," said Conor, and picked up the little white pig. It had pink eyes and a star on its forehead. "I wonder would it be a fairy pig?"

He thought of Biddy Connors of the Glen at home, who once had a cat with a star on its head. People for miles around swore it wasn't natural. Certainly to hear Biddy's cat sing in the moonlight and cut capers on the barn tops would make you wonder. And then it wouldn't eat anything but mushrooms and berries—though it drank all the milk it could get.

He stood up on the cart. Away up the road he could see Kathleen's black hair bobbing up and down and the donkey plodding along behind her, a sack of turf on one side of his back and a basket of eggs on the other. He couldn't make out where Bran was at all.

He dangled his legs and wondered if he should jump off and try and make his way up to them. A tall man with a pale face, wearing a green cloak, brushed against the cart. The next minute he was gone, taking the little white pig with him.

"He's stolen the pig," thought Conor in dismay, "and he has the look of the man we followed to the Fairy House on the Road to the Past."

The six black pigs saw that the white bonaveen was gone and they began to squeal in delight. The farmer, driving the cart, turned around to see what the turmoil was about. He had small, mean eyes and a tight mouth, and his voice was thin and high-pitched. "Riding in me fine cart. Get down ye young vagabond."

He made a drive with his whip at Conor, and the boy

jumped down and eased his way through the crowds. The farmer noticed that the little white pig was missing, and then the row started in earnest. He stood up, screeching in anger, lashing at his horse in an effort to find Conor. The animal reared high and then went tearing through the sheep, scattering everything wildly. The cart rocked and the pigs screamed in protest.

Conor's heart was thumping with fright. He tried to squeeze into the ditch on the side of the road. "Don't worry. Take shelter under my cloak and no harm will come to you." The man in the green cloak was beside Conor, sweeping him under his arm. The farmer drove past without seeing either of them.

The little white piglet, grunting in delight, was under the man's other arm. "Why did you steal him?" demanded Conor indignantly. "He doesn't belong to you."

"He belongs to no-one, but now and again he comes home to his own." The man was laughing and Conor noticed that his eyes were odd—one was blue and one was brown.

"Who are you?"

The wind whistled past in his ear, and he thought he heard the name Aengus, but when he looked up the man was tracing the star on the pig's forehead. "Would you like a ride on his back?" the man asked.

"Ride on the back of a bonaveen no bigger than my fists," thought Conor in annoyance. "Does the man take me for an omadaun?"

The pig jumped down and nestled beside Conor. The boy looked at it, and looked again. It had grown so big that it was now half as tall as himself. It grunted and pushed and somehow Conor's legs were across its back and he was riding along in style.

"I'm on the pig's back," he said and began to laugh. But the man in green was talking again. "Look between the pig's ears and you will see where you must go."

Conor looked. At first he could see only the road and the fair crowds. The sheep in front kicked up the white dust of the road, and Conor was almost blinded. When he opened his eyes again, he saw a mountain-pass and a thatched cottage near the top. Standing at the door was a baby with its mouth open and its eyes bulging. It was screaming its head off.

Conor stared and then looked at the man in green striding along beside him. He looked down again between the ears of the pig, but now all he could see was the snow blowing down, covering the people going the road to the fair.

"All I saw was a cottage and a crying baby," he said in disgust. The man in green chuckled. "Look in the pig's right ear and take what you'll find there."

Conor rooted and took out a small silver ball. He examined it delightedly and turned to thank his companion, but the man in green had vanished, and the pig was now trotting along beside the brown donkey.

Kathleen, chatting away in front to the egg woman and the turf boy, didn't see him. "Kathleen! Kathleen!" he called out.

She turned back sharply. "What are you doing riding an unfortunate pig. Get down at once and leave the animal be. I didn't think you were so lazy."

"She wouldn't believe me if I told her what happened," grumbled Conor, "but when I show her the silver ball, she'll get a surprise." He squeezed it between his fingers to make sure it was real. It bounced out of his hand, and he jumped down off the pig's back to recover it. When he looked around, the pig had vanished.

CHAPTER THIRTEEN

RED BIDDY

The snow was thick underfoot by the time they reached Bantry town. The egg woman and the turf boy had steady customers and in next to no time they had sold their wares. The turf boy got a bucket of water and a bunch of carrots for the donkey, and the butcher at the stall gave Bran a meaty bone.

Then they all went into a tent where a thin woman with red hair piled high on her head was pouring milky tea from a great kettle, and handing out piles of sandwiches.

"Grand strong tea, a penny a cup," she shouted. "Ham sandwiches, threepence each. Sweet juicy apple cake two-pence a slice."

The egg woman took two shillings out of her purse. "That's for eating and drinking for the four of us."

"Eating and drinking for four," said Red Biddy, then she looked up. "Wisha is it yourself, egg woman, and the turf boy? And who are the children?"

The children told her their names and their story. "We met your sister Huckster Peg and she told us to look out for you," said Conor. "We're anxious to get back the gold bracelet to disenchant the Swan Children, but the Tinker Chief won't give it up."

"I'll think of something," said Red Biddy. "Sit up to the table now and eat your fill."

She put them sitting at a well-scrubbed table in a corner beside a blind fiddler. He was drinking a cup of tea and eating a meat sandwich. He made room for the children, and bent down to scratch Bran's ears. The egg woman and the turf boy sat opposite.

"That's a grand little dog," he said, feeding Bran a piece of sandwich. "If I had a little dog I'd be made up."

"You would indeed," agreed the egg woman. In a few minutes Red Biddy came over with cups of milky tea and a plate of sandwiches. Then she brought over an apple cake with sugar on the top. The apples were sprinkled with cloves. "I've no liking for sweet things," she said, "but the apple cake is tasty and there's great nourishment in meat." She turned companionably to the fiddler. "Tell me, how are you doing at the fair?"

The fiddler held out his fingers. They were covered with chilblains. "I can't play a note and this is the biggest fair this side of Christmas."

Conor felt sorry for the fiddler and wondered if he could help. "What would my grannie say if she saw me playing the harmonica in the street," he thought, then he was ashamed of himself for his pride. He took a deep breath, and said in a rush, "I'll play for you, if you like."

"You play the fiddle," the old man was delighted.

"No, but I play the harmonica." Conor took it out of his pocket and laid it on the table.

"He's grand at it," said Kathleen eagerly. "He's the best harmonica player in the country."

"What are we waiting for," said the fiddler, standing up. Red Biddy bustled away and came back with a pile of sandwiches done up in brown paper. "You may need them later." She rooted in her pocket and brought out a silver ring. "It was given to me by the last King of the Tinkers. It is said whoever wears it will be King of them all. The Tinker Chief is mad to get it." She pressed it in Conor's palm. "Mind it now, it may come in useful."

Conor put the ring into his pocket and they all went out into the market square. All around them men and women were buying, selling, bartering. The brown donkey was standing at the stall of the gingerbread woman, and she was feeding him gingerbread cake. Bran was galloping around with a crowd of tinker dogs. Kathleen was glad to see they were another tribe.

Conor whispered in the ear of the fiddler. He nodded and they both struck up an old street ballad.

> "It's of a famous highwayman a story I will tell,
> His name was Willie Brennan and in Ireland he did dwell;
> And on the Kilworth mountains he commenced his bold career
> Where many a wealthy gentleman before him shook with fear.
>
> A brace of loaded pistols he carried day and night.
> He never robbed a poor man upon the king's highway,
> But what he'd take from the rich, like Turpin and Black Bess,
> He always did divide it with the people in distress."

The fiddler was singing and his voice quavered, but the notes of Conor's harmonica rang out clearly and sweetly. The noise and tumult of the fair died down, and people crowded around to listen. Kathleen shook the fiddler's old hat and pennies, three-penny bits, and even sixpences were thrown in. Soon it was almost full. Conor played on and on, and soon the whole fair was singing.

> "One night he robbed a packman by name of Pedlar Brown.
> They travelled on together till the day began to dawn.
> The pedlar seeing his money gone, likewise his watch and chain,
> He at once encountered Brennan and he robbed him back again."

"Who's singing about robbers? There's the young thief who stole my pig." An angry voice broke through the song, and there was the mean-faced farmer pushing his way through the crowd. His face was red with anger, and he waved his whip furiously. "Out of my way till I flay him alive."

Conor thrust the hat at the fiddler. "The money is all yours. It will help you." Then he was gone racing through the fair. The farmer tried to follow, but the egg woman was standing in front of him. Roughly he pushed her aside, but the turf boy was blocking his path. He waved his whip, and the crowd melted away. Then out between his legs shot a small white pig. It had a star on its forehead. The farmer stumbled and fell to the ground. But he jumped up shouting almost at once.

"Hee-haw," said the donkey. "Where are you, Bran? We're in trouble."

The farmer made a drive at the donkey, but the animal shot out his front hooves and the farmer went stumbling away. He was flaying his whip wildly around him, when Bran and a crowd of tinker dogs came galloping up.

"Let's chase the mean old farmer out of town," barked Bran, and the tinker dogs bit and snapped and snarled at the farmer. The snow was blowing in his eyes and he couldn't see where he was going. He leaped in the air and went running zig-zag across the fair with the pack at his heels. He jumped up into his red cart and lashed his horse and the black pigs in the back squealed with temper. The cart lurched and the horse began to gallop. "I'm going home," the farmer shouted crossly. "'Tis the unluckiest fair I was ever at. Not a bit of luck did I have since I stole that white pig."

The tinker dogs chased the cart down the road, but Bran came racing back. "He's gone and good riddance," he barked.

"Hee-haw," brayed the donkey. "He won't trouble us again."

"The fair is nearly over, we'd best be on our way," said Kathleen. And they took the road west to Gougane Barra.

CHAPTER FOURTEEN

THE CHANGELING

For the length of the afternoon they travelled. Smoke rose from the chimneys of the cottages on the mountainside, and light gleamed in every window. The road was narrow and jagged with rocks. Once they stopped by a stream to eat their sandwiches and drink the water, but though the snow had stopped falling, an icy wind was blowing up before them, and they quickly went on their way again.

Kathleen pulled her thin coat around her and peered anxiously through the short twilight. "It looks as if we're going into some kind of a ravine."

"A pass of some kind, I'd say," agreed Conor. Kathleen was sitting on the donkey's back, but Conor was plodding along and he felt tired and miserable.

The snow underfoot was freezing hard and the wind was blowing sleet from the mountain-tops. "I wonder would it be the Pass of Keimaneigh?"

"Hee-haw," said the donkey, "I'm lame and I can't go any further." He stood still and Kathleen climbed down off his back. "I think there's a stone in his hoof," said Conor, and he bent to try to dislodge it with a penknife.

Bran was jumping around trying to keep his spirits up. "Why do donkeys have long ears and short legs?" he barked, but the donkey was too weary to answer riddles.

"Because that's the long and the short of them," barked Bran, and the donkey threw back his head and roared "Hee-haw, shut up or I'll kick you into the next field."

"Even the animals are quarrelling," said Kathleen, almost in tears. "What will we do, Conor?"

Away in the distance someone shouted, "Hullo there!" A

light bobbed up and down and drew near. It was a thin young man with a shock of red hair and kind blue eyes.

"I was out looking for some sheep when I heard the racket the donkey and the dog were making. What are you children doing out at this time of the night, and it so bad?"

"We're going to Gougane Barra," said Conor listlessly. The snow and the sleet had him both famished and sleepy.

"You're off the road, and it's a good six miles away," said the young man. He ran his thin fingers through his hair and thought hard a moment. "You'd best come with me. I'm a shoemaker and my home isn't a stone's throw away."

Bran trotted along after him, up the pass. Conor and Kathleen stumbled behind and the donkey limped as best he could.

They stopped at a small thatched cottage near the top of the pass. Conor recognised it immediately. It was the place he had seen, riding the white pig on the road to the fair.

And there was the cross baby, crying its head off at the half door. A few hens and ducks scattered in alarm, when they saw the donkey and the dog, and a kind, good-natured woman, pushing back strands of her hair, came out. She wiped soapy hands in her apron and tried to lift the baby, but it only screamed louder and flailed the air with its legs. The shoemaker had difficulty in making himself heard above the din.

"I found the children below the pass. They're worn out with cold and hunger. Looking for Gougane Barra they are but too weary to go another foot. Take them and the dog inside and I'll put the donkey into the barn and give him a feed. His hoof needs seeing to."

The thin young man led the donkey away and his wife brought the children into the kitchen and began to dry their clothes. She succeeded in catching the baby and putting him sitting in a high chair. He remained still a moment and then threw a blue-delph mug on the floor. It crashed in a dozen pieces, and at this the baby screamed so loudly that the woman had to lift him down again. She sighed wearily.

"I don't know what's the matter with him. He used to be

the best baby in Co. Cork, but now there's no living with him. He does nothing but cry, night, noon and morning."

The shoemaker was back again, shaking the sleet from his coat. "I've seen to the donkey," he said, above the roars of the baby. "He's eating a feed of straw and I've fixed the hoof. He'll be as right as rain in the morning."

Kathleen gave the baby her finger; he only put it in his mouth and bit it. Then he pushed Kathleen away and went on screaming. "I'll whistle and it might quieten him," sighed the shoemaker. "Sometimes a bit of music is the only thing that soothes him down."

"You're worn out," said the woman, and she tried to croon a lullaby. At this the baby raised such a howl that Kathleen put her hands to her ears and Bran began to bark.

Conor looked around desperately. Then he took the harmonica out of his pocket. "Look I'll play him a tune. Maybe he'll like that." At this Bran stopped barking and the baby fixed him with two sharp blue eyes, as if to say, "Get on with it. Hurry up about it."

Conor sat on a stool and the baby climbed up beside him. He played a jig and a reel, and then a tune he had learned from the little men in the bog, and when he had finished the baby gurgled and clapped its hands together. The shoemaker and his wife looked at each other in delight. "He liked it. It's the first time in months he's smiled. Maybe he'll remain quiet while I make the supper." And the woman began to bustle around mashing potatoes and adding hot milk and a fistful of chopped onions.

Kathleen and Conor were happy. Outside the storm was shrieking around the eaves, but inside it was warm and comfortable. The shoemaker and his wife were grand homely people, and even the cross baby had quietened down, only pulling Kathleen's hair now and again and pinching Conor's arm. Finally, worn out with such diversion, he fell asleep, and the woman of the house settled him in a wicker basket beside the fire.

She tidied the room, raked the fire in the sign of the cross and turned down the lamp. Bran was snoring in the corner.

"Now I think it's time we all went to bed," she said. "I haven't had a proper night's rest in months, with the baby so troublesome. Would you children sleep on the settle near the fire. It's warm and comfortable. We have only one bedroom."

Kathleen was half asleep. "That would be grand, ma'am, and we'll keep an eye on the baby."

The woman turned down the light, and gave the children a rug to put over them. "I don't like leaving the baby in the basket beside the fire, for I'm afraid he'll burn himself. But lately it's the only place he'll sleep."

The children lay down on the settle—one at each end, because it was long and narrow, and they all slept peacefully until just before daybreak. Then Kathleen woke with a start. Bran was at the baby's basket, growling into the baby's ear.

Angrily Kathleen shook Conor. "Will you look at that dog of yours disturbing the baby and he so peaceful. Now we're for it again."

The baby fell out of the cradle and stumbled to its feet. It opened its mouth wide, and Kathleen braced herself for a scream, but instead he said in a cross old man's voice, "Bran is the only one amongst you with a grain of sense. Will you for goodness sake make me a good strong cup of tea. I'm fed up with milk and baby food."

Half scared out of her wits, Kathleen began to build up the fire and boil the kettle. Conor was staring at the baby as if he couldn't believe his eyes. "I—I didn' t think you could talk. You're only a baby."

The terrible child sniffed. "Didn't you indeed? And as for being a baby I'm older by far than the pair of you put together. Hurry up with the tea, Kathleen."

Kathleen held out a cup of tea, and the baby grabbed it and gulped it down. "You are—you must be a Changeling," she whispered.

"Well, so what if I am. I wanted to learn to make and mend properly and the man of the house here has the name of being the best shoemaker in County Cork. I'm a shoemaker myself, you see. So I came along."

Kathleen held on to the side of the settle for support. She

couldn't believe what she saw. The baby was changing before her eyes. Little hairs were sprouting out of the side of his face. And now he had whiskers. His hair was growing long and grey, and his baby shoes were curling up at the toes.

Conor thought of the shoemaker and his wife, asleep in the next room, and pinched himself to make sure he wasn't dreaming. "What—what did you do with their baby?" he whispered.

The Changeling took up the shoemaker's pipe and lit it with a red sod. "Oh he's having the time of his life with the Good People. Of course when he comes home, he won't remember a word, but people will always say he's a bit clever

in the head. He'll be a great musician too when he grows up." He puffed contemptuously at his pipe. "Small blame to him and the company he's been keeping for the past few months."

Kathleen poured out another cup of tea. She thought it as well to humour the Changeling, though a plan was forming in her mind. "When are you going back to your own people?" she asked.

"Just now, if you'll give me a lift." To listen to the Changeling you'd know it wasn't a request but a demand. "I've been a baby so long I've almost forgotten how to walk. Besides I can't run around the mountains in baby clothes."

"If we take you with us will you help us find the tinkers?" asked Kathleen.

"It's the only thing you can do if you want to get away from here," put in Conor.

The Changeling knocked the shreds of tobacco into the fire and tapped the pipe on to the palm of his hand. He looked so funny that Kathleen wanted to laugh, but instead she said in a bossy tone. "You can ride on the donkey's back. Is it a bargain?"

"Oh very well," said the Changeling crossly. "I'll do my part and you do yours. But after that we each go our way."

CHAPTER FIFTEEN

THE WHITE CAT AGAIN

The fire had died very low. The old clock on the mantelpiece tick-tocked and then struck five. Outside the wind was silent and the stars were dimming, but dawn had not yet come. On tip-toes Conor and Kathleen crept out and after them Bran with the Changeling stumbling along holding on to the dog's ears.

Conor went over to the barn and opened it. The donkey was shaking himself awake and the hens and ducks in the corner waddled out after him. They went croaking up to the Changeling. They seemed to be saying, "Good-bye."

The little man looked glumly at the children. "Will you for goodness sake hurry up before it's too late."

"We're hurrying," said Kathleen crossly. She lifted the Changeling up on the donkey's back and she climbed up. Conor was going back to the cottage.

"Where do you think you're going," demanded Kathleen.

"To collect my cap," said Conor in an apologetic tone. "I've forgotten it."

Kathleen got down again, slipped on the ice and with a sigh picked herself up again. "For goodness sake stay where you are. I'll get it for you. You're so noisy you'll only bring the house down about your ears."

The Changeling coughed and wagged his ears, suddenly grown long and pointed. "If you're not quick I'm going on without you," he shouted peevishly.

Softly Kathleen crept back into the still kitchen. Then her eyes almost popped out of her head in amazement. There in the cradle sleeping peacefully was a baby. A large fat baby, something like the Changeling, only younger and nicer. It had its thumb in its mouth and every now and then it gave a little gurgle of laughter as if it were still playing with the little fairy men in the woodland glades.

Kathleen tucked the blankets around it and stood looking down. The baby crowed in its sleep, and she thought of how glad the shoemaker and his wife would be to have their nice jolly baby back again. "I wonder will they realise they've been minding a Changeling, all this time," she thought, "or will they imagine the baby was cross because he was teething, or something. Ah well, I'll never know."

She took Conor's cap from the nail behind the door and gave a last look around the cosy kitchen. "I'd like to leave a note of thanks. But it would be too hard to explain. Perhaps we'll meet again some day."

She closed the door quietly behind her and went out and got up on the donkey's back, behind Conor and the Changeling. The donkey kicked his heels and went zig-zagging down the mountainside, and Bran ran alongside.

The path was treacherous, and here and there thin sheets of ice covered the drifts. "If the donkey falls, we're finished," thought Conor desperately. "I wonder should I get down and lead him." He looked back to see where was Bran. The dog was almost covered in snow and he could hardly walk.

As if he could read Conor's thoughts, the Changeling snapped out. "Use your head. Didn't you find something in the white pig's ear on the road to the fair?"

Conor rooted in his pocket and pulled out the silver ball. It seemed to come alive in his hand, quivered and with a leap was gone skimming down the mountains. It cut the snow and ice in two—and now there was a soft green path. Bran barked in delight and the Changeling chortled. The donkey gave a great leap and Conor and Kathleen shot up in the air and went rolling, rolling down to the bottom of the pass.

As they picked themselves up, dawn was breaking. Neither was hurt, but both were wet and cross. They looked around, but there was no sign of the donkey, the dog or the Changeling.

"He's given us the slip, the little wretch," said Conor angrily. "And taken Bran and the donkey with him." He looked around for the silver ball, but couldn't find it. Kathleen shook the snow off her coat and tossed back her hair. "I'm surprised the Changeling didn't keep his word, and we after helping him."

Conor sighed. "You can never trust a Changeling. They're up to all sorts of tricks."

Kathleen nodded. She was so disappointed she could have cried, but she held her head high and said very loudly. "Ah well, we'll find our own way to Gougane Barra." She hoped the Changeling was around somewhere and could hear what she said.

Conor picked up a willow wand and began to peel it. He tried to blow through it, and then threw it away.

"I only hope we find the brown donkey," he said mournfully.

"After all we only have the loan of him. I wouldn't like to lose him. We'll probably never see Bran again either. I don't know what my grannie will say."

The sun was coming up and the frost was melting, but here and there were treacherous pools of water, and a stream that was running high gushed across the road. They climbed over a hedge and into a field. Away in the distance they could see a woman picking twigs. She beckoned to them and they began to run towards her. They stumbled over a tuft of grass and were suddenly weak with hunger.

"We're on the hungry grass," said Conor, pulling Kathleen after him. "My grannie says if you don't get off it you die of hunger."

They started to run, but now they were going round in circles. Conor stopped and thought hard. "My grannie says if you look at the ground and put one foot in front of the other you walk in a straight line."

It seemed to take them ages to do this, but somehow they were across a gap, and into a field where the woman was bent over tugging at a branch on the ground. She straightened up as they came near. Her shawl covered all her face, except her eyes which were bright and sharp. "Are you in trouble?" she asked.

"We almost died on the hungry grass," explained Conor mournfully. "We're still starving."

The woman walked on before them, hitching her shawl around her like a tent. "Follow me," she called over her shoulder, "and I'll look after you." She laughed in a curious manner, but the children were too hungry to pay much attention.

Behind the trees was a neat little cottage with lace curtains on the window and a door painted red. "It has the look of Horseshoe Cottage," said Kathleen to herself. "I wonder are there any leprechauns about." She giggled and followed the woman inside.

A three-legged pot on the fire was bubbling with porridge, but the big black kettle was empty. "I'm going to the well to get water," said the woman, "and maybe I'll get you a few of my special herbs." She eyed them slyly and said, "Don't move until I get back."

Thankfully the children sat down by the fire. Conor was so hungry that he put his finger into the pot of porridge, but Kathleen slapped his wrist. "Don't attempt to do that. Mind your manners. What would the nice woman say?"

"Nice woman how are you. She's a Witch." The children were so startled at the voice that they jumped. Seated on the window sill was the White Cat.

"It's Báinín," said Kathleen. "However did you get here and what are you talking about?"

The Cat jumped on to the floor beside them. "I was on my travels," she said loftily, "when I met the Changeling. He told me you were in trouble. The Witch thought you would be destroyed on the hungry grass. Now she's up to some other mischief."

Kathleen was very annoyed. "The Changeling vanished. He ran away and took the donkey and the dog with him too."

The White Cat looked bored. She licked her shoulder and rubbed her nose before answering. "I thought anyone with a grain of sense would realise that the Changeling had to get home before dawn broke. You'll see the dog and donkey soon enough."

Conor edged nervously towards the door. "We'd best get away before the Witch comes back. I'd rather not meet her again."

The Cat looked at him in amusement. Then she stood up, and stretched her paws. "Oh you might as well stand your ground. Running away from that old one will get you nowhere."

"Who's an old woman?" The Witch had thrown back her shawl and now she came storming in. The White Cat leaped gracefully on to the top of the dresser, and the children jumped up on the table in terror. The Cat spat viciously at the Witch. "Leave the children alone, or it will be the worse for you."

"I turned my stepchildren into swans," screamed the Witch, waltzing around in rage. "I'll turn you all into beetles and crush you under my feet."

The Cat hissed and jumped down. She faced the Witch with her back arched and her tail as stiff as a ramrod. "Very well. We'll have a battle of wits and turn ourselves into this and that. But whoever turns back into her own shape first loses the battle."

CHAPTER SIXTEEN

KING OF THE TINKERS

The Witch struck first. With a scream she turned into a vicious black dog with smouldering eyes, and caught the Cat by the throat. Quick as lightning the Cat turned into a stick and began to beat the dog. Then the Witch was a woodpecker, eating the stick, now the Cat was a raven picking the woodpecker's eyes. The Witch was a huge red fox attacking the raven, but the Cat was a terrible wild boar, and for a while fox and boar fought savagely. Then the Witch was a ball of fire, scorching and burning the boar, but the Cat was a stream of water that gushed down and quenched the fire.

Smoke rose in the kitchen and when it cleared the Witch was cowering on the floor, wet and miserable. The Cat jumped up on the table beside the trembling children. "Fire is powerful," said the Cat, "but nothing can destroy water. Leave this house and never return."

The brown donkey was coming up to the cottage door as the Witch flew past. She scratched his coat with her dirty talons, but the donkey kicked sideways, and the Witch went sailing up up in the sky until she was lost to sight.

While the children climbed down from the table Bran came loping in. His ears hung down and he looked hang-dog and ashamed.

Conor was still so nervous he turned on his dog. "You're a nice fellow going off like that and leaving us. Only for the White Cat we were destroyed."

"It wasn't my fault," whined Bran, and the Cat twitched her whiskers and said loftily, "Dogs have no sense of dignity. Sit down and eat your porridge."

Bran and the White Cat sat on either sides of the fire and dozed. Outside the brown donkey thoughtfully nibbled a few

thistles and spoke severely to a spider who was trying to eat her husband.

When the children had finished their breakfast they rose to go. The donkey came to the window and put in his head, hee-hawing loudly.

"The tinkers are arriving below in Gougane Barra," said the Cat without removing her gaze from the flames. "The donkey says you had better hurry."

Outside the door the children climbed up on the donkey's

back and Bran went racing before them. Kathleen turned to take one last look at the cottage where so much had happened. But all she could see now was a giant oak tree and something that might have been the cat's eyes glinting from the branches.

The donkey went at a great gallop. He leaped over hedges and splashed across streams, and twice the children were nearly knocked off his back by trailing branches blown down by the storm.

The sun was shining down on the lake and four swans were swimming around, as they came to Gougane Barra. A little distance away they could see the tinkers, shouting and singing as they unyoked their carts and caravans.

The children got off the donkey's back and he wandered off to nibble a patch of green grass. Bran plunged into the lake and Conor said in dismay. "He'll frighten off the swans." But the swans paid no attention and the dog came swimming back with a trout in his mouth.

"He's brought us our dinner," said Kathleen in delight, and while Conor gathered up twigs and bits of turf to make a fire, she cleaned the fish. She rubbed two twigs together, a trick she had learned with the tinkers, and soon a bright fire was blazing. In the corner of a field they found a few potatoes. They roasted the fish and potatoes and when they had finished they lay down on the grass and fell fast asleep.

The donkey, nuzzling their faces, woke them up. The short winter's day was over, and the moon was sailing out from behind the hills. Up the fields they could see the tinker fire and around it the Chief and the tribe sprawling and eating.

"Where's Bran?" wondered Conor, rubbing his eyes. Then he looked around, and there was the dog trotting over the grass and perched on his back the Changeling.

"You came back," said Kathleen in wonder.

"I always keep my word," said the Changeling sharply. "Hee-haw," said the donkey, "he promised to lead you to the tinkers," but Bran barked, "It isn't time yet."

For a little while they were silent. The children were still half-asleep, and the Changeling seemed to be waiting. The night was filled with sound, as if all the winds in the world were singing among the branches of silver and gold. Overhead the four swans went winging their way to the mountains. The Changeling looked less like a dried up little man, and more like a creature of wind and mist, moonlight and shadow, which indeed he was. He spoke and even his voice was gentle. And then Kathleen knew why the fairies are sometimes called the Good People, and sometimes the Gentle Folk.

"This is an enchanted moment, children. Make a wish."

Conor's voice was subdued. His eyes were on the tinker encampment. "I wish—I wish that we got back the gold bracelet and that the swan children were disenchanted forever."

The Changeling looked at Kathleen. In her thin coat and broken shoes she looked lost and lonely. "I wish that someday, someplace, I might have a home of my own and never again be travelling the roads."

A shout of laughter shattered the night's magic. The Tinker Chief had jumped to his feet, waving a mug in his hand. As he did so Kathleen remembered where she had seen it all before. It was on the Road to the Future.

"This is the time you must face the Tinker Chief," said the Changeling, "and get the bracelet back," but when the children looked again all they saw was a handful of leaves swirling in the wind, in the place where the Changeling had been standing. Somehow they were sitting on the donkey's back and with Bran alongside, they went racing into the encampment.

The tinkers let out a roar of delight when they saw them. "It's Kathleen back," yelled the Chief, "and she's brought a donkey and a dog. Maybe the boy will stay with us too."

"We came to get the bracelet," shouted Conor. "It doesn't belong to you."

"Come and get it," roared the Chief, dancing in delight. The tinkers were lifting the children off the donkey's back, but Bran was running around, snapping at their heels, and the dogs of the tribe were joining in the fun.

"Get them down. Capture the donkey. Get the dogs out

of the way," screamed the Chief. The donkey kicked out to the left and the right and clods of earth rose up in the air and everyone scattered.

In her excitement Kathleen stood up on the donkey's back and shouted. "Give up the bracelet."

"Come down and get it," shouted the Chief, then with a dash of bravado he took it off his arm and tossed it high in the air. From under his feet Bran leaped high and caught it in his mouth—then he was racing across the encampment towards the mountain.

The donkey went flying after him, with the children clinging on for dear life. The Tinker Chief was chasing them. Then Conor suddenly remembered the silver ring Red Biddy had given him at the fair. He rooted in his pocket, pulled it out, and threw it back, shouting, "Whoever catches it will be King of the Tinkers."

The Tinker Chief bent down to pick it up, and all the others following after fell on top of him.

CHAPTER SEVENTEEN

THE END OF THE SEARCH

The cry of the tinkers grew fainter as the donkey moved away, and faintly Kathleen could catch the words. "At last! I'm the King of the Tinkers."

The donkey scrambled up the mountainside, with the children clinging on to his back. His hooves dislodged small stones and they were cascading down. "Be careful, Bran," shouted Conor, but when he looked around there was no sign of the dog.

At the top of the mountains, purple gorse and heather grew on flat land, and there was a brown mountain pool with four swans swimming around. Beyond the pool was a flat topped rock, running into the side of the hill. As the children got down off the donkey's back, they saw a man with a flying green cloak, with a little dog trotting by his side, come around the side of the rock.

The moon came over the hills and now the children could see the man and dog go to the lake's edge.

"It's Bran," said Conor. "It's Bran and the man in the green cloak with him."

"It's Aengus and the Swan Children," said Kathleen and tears came into her eyes.

As they watched Aengus bent and took the gold bracelet from Bran's mouth. The swans went gliding over the pool to the rushy bank, and Aengus bent down and in turn slipped the bracelet over the swans' necks. The moon dipped, and when it came out again they saw a pool of light and five radiant figures—Aengus and beside him three boys and a girl. The Swan Children looked across the mountains and raised their hands in farewell. Then with Aengus by their side they turned and walked into the face of the rock and vanished from sight.

"At last the Children of Lir are disenchanted," said Kathleen. "It's the end of our search."

"And the last of the gold bracelet," sighed Conor. "Ah well, it wasn't ours in the first place."

Bran was swimming across the pool, and now he was beside the children, shaking the water from his coat. Around his neck was a collar of gold.

"Aengus sent us back the bracelet, only now it's so big it makes a collar for Bran," said Conor, awe in his voice.

"Real old gold. Studded with rubies and diamonds," said Kathleen, kneeling beside the dog and turning the collar around on his neck. Yes, there were still the curious little animals carved on the collar, only now they had eyes and tails of precious stones.

For the last time they climbed up on the donkey's back and went back the long road they had come.

They stopped off at the shop of Huckster Peg to return the brown donkey and to tell their story. The Ballad Singer and the Rosy Woman of the Caravan were there before them.

"Your wishes came true," said the Ballad Singer. "The collar of gold is worth a king's ransom. You'll never again know a poor day."

Kathleen looked forlorn. "I wished for a home of my own, but the wish didn't come true." She looked at Conor but he was feeding carrots to the brown donkey and didn't hear her.

"Stay with me," invited Huckster Peg. "I could do with a smart girl like yourself. I'll teach you how to make toffee-apples and peggy's leg."

"Come travelling the roads with me," said the Rosy Woman. "It's a grand life in a caravan. You meet everyone and see everything that happens."

But the Ballad Singer shook his head. "Leave the child be. She'll come into her own yet."

Next morning the Rosy Woman bundled the children,

the Ballad Singer and Bran into her caravan to take them part of the road home.

"Hee-haw," said the donkey as they drove away. "I'm glad to be home, but I enjoyed our adventures. Hee-haw."

And this time the children knew what he was saying and shouted, "Good-bye, brown donkey. Good-bye."

At the top of the lake road, the Rosy Woman stopped her caravan and they all climbed down. "I'll go no further, children," she said, "but whenever I'm passing I'll call and see you."

"I'll say good-bye too," said the Ballad Singer, "for I'd sooner walk than ride." He turned to the children. "You've made your fortune, but better than that you've made friends—and friends are something that money can't buy. All the days of your life you will remember your adventures and the marvel of it all. Good-bye."

"Good-bye," called the children and they waved until he was out of sight.

The sun was going down behind the mountains and the road was full of dim golden lights and queer long shadows when the children came up to the cottage. The old woman was waiting at the door.

"I knew ye were coming back. All night long I dreamt that Bran was coming over the hills with a wonderful collar of gold around his neck. But better than that I knew that Conor and Kathleen were coming home too." She bent down and kissed the little girl. 'Welcome, Kathleen. This is your home. Never again will you go travelling the roads."

They were moving into the cottage when the little dog pointed his ears and barked. From the distance came a shout. Conor looked at Kathleen, and she at him.

"The tinkers. The tinkers are on the roads. We'll see them pass by."

Down by the side of the mountains straggled the carts and caravans. At their head was the Tinker Chief. His gold earrings flashed, his black hair curled down his back, his jacket was gorgeous and around his head he wore a scarlet scarf.

He waved to the children and on his finger was the silver ring of the Tinker Chief.

" Are you coming with us, Kathleen," he called.

She shook her head a little sadly. "I'm staying with Conor and his grannie. I'm tired of travelling around. But maybe someday I'll meet you all again."

"Whenever we're passing we'll call in. Maybe someday we'll settle down too. Now I must make the rounds of Ireland to tell them all that I am the King of the Tinkers." And he began to sing :

> "Oh at last I'm the King of the Tinkers bold,
> And I walk with a ring of silver and gold.
> I travel the roads with a careless swagger
> Afraid of no man, king or beggar."

And with a great laugh the tribe joined in,

> "Oh he's the King of the Tinkers bold
> And at every fair will his deeds be told."

"He got his wish at last. He's the King of the Tinkers," said Conor. "I'm glad."

The tinkers passed on. As the children watched them go around the bend of the road, Bran barked plaintively, and they sighed. The sigh spoke of relief certainly, but perhaps too it spoke of regret. The great adventure was over.

Then Kathleen and Conor with the faithful dog at their heels raced home.